Pose for Me
Halli Starling

Halli Starling Books

Contents

Also by Halli Starling   1

Author's Note   3

Content Warnings   4

Dedication   5

1. Chapter 1   6

2. Chapter 2   12

3. Chapter 3   21

4. Chapter 4   31

5. Chapter 5   41

6. Chapter 6   51

7. Chapter 7   63

8. Chapter 8   76

9. Chapter 9   92

10. Chapter 10   108

About the author   117

Also by Halli Starling

Wilderwood

Twelfth Moon

Ask Me For Fire

A Brighter, Darker Art

When He Beckons

The Way We Wind

Always There For You

Coup de Coeur

(Oracle, Tailor, Curator trilogy, Book 1)

Venor

(The Werewolf Novels, Book 1)

Demimonde

(Oracle, Tailor, Curator trilogy, Book 2)

Verto

(The Werewolf Novels, Book 2; coming late 2025)

Book 3 in the Oracle, Tailor, Curator

INCARNER

Coming 2026

Author's Note

I released this ebook for free in hopes that it would be picked up by anyone wanting a breezy, feel-good queer romance novella. At the time of this writing (February 2025), the United States government is run by a tinpot dictator and a South African billionaire who are working in tandem to dismantle protections for anyone who isn't white/male/cis/Christian/straight. Queer art is more important than ever, and because I'm putting this ebook out for free, it's my hope that you share it with others. (But please don't pirate books; only share what you have explicit permission for.) Maybe, if you're reading this in the future, we've managed to beat fascism back. I hope that's true.

If you want a paperback version of this book, it will be available via most major retailers and in my Etsy shop (booksbyhalli.etsy.com).

Take care of each other.

Content Warnings

- Language

- On-page, detailed sex scenes

- Discussions of addiction

- Mention of parent death

For Lou, this book's first reader and a very kind, funny person I'm lucky enough to call *friend*.

Chapter 1

HOLLAND

The bird staring at Holland was wearing an eyepatch. A tiny, bright blue eyepatch. The other beady eye was trained on him with the accuracy of a sniper. And it kept staring at him.

Holland fussed with his tripod one more time, knowing it was as stable as the ground under his feet, but he had to break that eye contact *somehow*. *Unnerving* didn't touch it with a ten-foot pole.

"Are you all set, Mr. Mauerbach?" he asked. His client was wearing a three-piece suit, the blue of his tie a perfect match for the parrot's eyepatch. It wasn't the strangest client he'd ever had, but it was higher on the list than most.

"We're good," Mr. Mauerbach replied. "I appreciate you letting us into your studio. So many photographers get antsy about Peaches here. Which isn't fair."

The bird was still staring at him. Well, at least it was looking toward the camera. But his client was pleasant enough. Had been since the day he'd reached out via email (typed in ALL CAPS but strangely polite, as if an aging blueblood lord with hearing issues still had impeccable manners). And Holland had seen all manner of animals come in - dogs, cats, a few lizards, more than a fair share of snakes. He'd even shot the images for the zoo's charity calendar fundraiser.

But there was something about this bird.

Holland shook it off as Mr. Mauerbach struck a Napoleon-esque pose, a closed fist over his heart, legs staggered. "Ready?" Holland asked.

"Ready!"

The word came from the parrot and not his human client and Holland could only laugh.

When the photos were done, he let Michael, who ran the small studio's appointment book and phone line, deal with Mr. Mauerbach's payment and photo pick-up instructions. Holland prided himself on offering physical portrait packs in an age of digital-only, and he'd drawn in a healthy revolving door of clients that way. Older and younger, since like vinyl, mixtapes, and overalls, everything old was new again. He'd been around long enough to see trends from his own high school days resurface, but now everyone wore scrunchies and scuffed Chucks and he thought the world was better for a more gender inclusive and neutral way of thinking.

And Chucks were timeless. Scrunchies he'd had to be convinced into by his ten-year-old niece, but she'd been right; they did keep his shoulder-length dark blonde hair out of his face but didn't hurt like those little snappy band things he spent more time breaking than actually using.

Holland's ass barely hit his desk chair before Michael was poking his head of red curls around the office door. "Need anything before I take off?"

Holland shook his head. "All good. Thanks for handling Mr. Mauerbach. Bit of a character."

"Honestly, I think it's his bird that runs the show," Michael replied while picking faded gray paint off the worn door jamb. "Anyways, cool. I'll make sure the front light's off so people don't go banging on the door trying to see if you're still open. I'll leave you with this and head out into the night."

Holland stifled a laugh. Michael was the grandson of his god-mother's best friend, and since Gamma lived with Holland, and Daisy was always over, that meant Michael was usually nearby. It had only made sense to hire the younger man, whose very shiny but *too shiny* English Lit degree wasn't exactly cracking open the doors of job opportunities. And iron-will Daisy would never let her grandson be a black mark on her reputation, so Holland had no doubt from day one Michael would be a hell of a worker. Daisy could be a lot sometimes, but Michael had grown into a kind, sometimes goofy guy with a good eye and a natural charm that eased even the most angry of customers.

Holland took the neatly folded note from Michael, saw the name "Laurent", and tried not to get too excited. Laurent Oliver (who Holland had never gotten the nerve to ask if his parents hated him, because *why* that name?) ran the online marketing department for a fancy firm and was easily his biggest client. CEO headshots, department group photos, "fun run" action shots. Laurent had brought him the zoo job and many, many others that helped keep the lights on and both he and Michael paid, so Holland immedi-ately reached for his phone.

Michael left with a wave while the line rang in his ear.

"Holland Swisher, you lucky son of a bitch."

Holland laughed. "What did I do to you?"

"Oh no, it's what I'm about to do for you." Laurent had a East Coast harshness to his voice, situated somewhere between Brook-lyn and Boston, and Holland had always secretly liked the sound of his voice. Laurent was straight and married but campy enough to keep up with Holland's "brat pack", aka the group of college friends

Holland went out with once a month or so. He'd invited Laurent a few times and the man from an opposite coast and perpendicular sexuality to all of them had fit right in. His dad jokes might be met with eye rolls and sharp elbows to the ribs, but for a straight guy, Laurent was all right.

"So I need another charity calendar," Laurent said. "And I need it like yesterday. The fancy bankers and business folks who replaced the old guard on the Color Run board wants to do something big. So, I need you."

He flashed back to that bird's beady little eye and shuddered. "It's not birds, is it?"

"Don't like birds, Holland?"

"Give me grief later, but give me the details now." *Including the monetary aspect.*

"I finally understand why Rowan calls you grouchy chic," Laurent mumbled before clearing his throat. "So, charity calendar. Photos. Yesterday. Aka as soon as possible. How free are you this week?"

Holland did a quick set of calculations in his head. The charity calendars were always good money, and it was just after Halloween. The ever-increasing early holiday creep meant he'd cave to the invisible pressure of already thinking about gifts...so yes, of course he'd do it. But that didn't mean he couldn't drive a hard bargain. "There's a rush order fee, Laurent. Non-negotiable."

"I already told the board that and they're in. But I have a feeling you'd do this for no extra money."

Holland perked up at that. Anything but birds. Or more family photos with scowling grandkids in new clothes they clearly hated and overbearing adults trying to keep toddlers from squirreling away at first opportunity. Those days were like a circus and it was all Holland could do from collapsing the minute he got home. People forgot about him behind the camera. They ignored his advice, made unreasonable demands, asked for discounts because they were totally going to give him "exposure."

Sure, Jan, and he was a sugar glider.

And slowly, over the years, he felt his love of the work — the *art* of taking photographs, the light, the composition, the moment's peace before closing the shutter — had begun to dwindle away. Wearing him down, until he was a nub of who he'd once been.

Holland leaned back in his chair and let his head tip back until he was staring at water-stained ceiling tiles. "Okay," he said with way more emotion than he meant to.

"Remember those old 'Hunks of the City' calendars? Well, the board wants to revive them, but make them inclusive. So you get to photograph hot guys for a week, get paid handsomely to do so, and the holiday Color Run makes money."

Holland frowned at that one. "I mean yeah, I remember those. But I thought our generation was a little more aware of how objectifying they are."

Laurent actually laughed. "Oh, buddy, trust me, I get it. But Mr. January through December signed up for this readily. Their ringleader, this guy Alexander, was the one to approach the board. Apparently a bunch of the guys do the run every year and wanted to help out, raise some money for the kids cancer charities with the holidays approaching. If they're willing to be objectified for a good cause and it was *their* idea? I'd take it and run, so the board did."

The hackles that had gone up immediately at the thought of photographing someone only begrudgingly willing flattened a little. "Okay, fine. They're all on board. Why me?"

"Aside from getting to stare at hot guys for work?"

Holland held his tongue, mostly to keep from snapping out a sharp reply. Laurent was a decent person, even if he had the type of personality that was clearly meant for marketing: slick, smooth, bit of a guy's guy. But Laurent's biggest sin wasn't that he was straight, but that he was the kind of straight that thought every gay guy was, deep down, a slavering beast in it for a nice set of pecs, taut stomach, and big dick. And he meant it in the way he thought a lot of straight guys were objectifying bastards. Equal opportunity grossness all around. Some gays *were* like that. Some straights *were* like that with the opposite sex. But it left people like him out in the cold a bit.

You need the money. These guys volunteered themselves. Don't over-think it. Holland sort of hated himself the moment he leaned forward, elbows pressed hard into his desk's top, and said, "All right. Send me all the details and I'll make sure to be ready."

Chapter 2

HOLLAND

Holland found his godmother in the backyard, back turned to the patio door, the thin, snaking line of her earbuds curving down until they disappeared into the pocket of her fuzzy cardigan. Once through the glass door, he was careful to step far to the left, in her eye line.

Gamma caught his wave after only a second, and as she straightened and pulled a glove off to pat him on the cheek, Holland said, "I can't believe that thing is still flowering, as cold as it is anymore."

Gamma touched a soft pink rose petal with her gloved finger. "This thing will probably be here long after we're both gone. Unless global warming gets her." She paused, head cocked. "Global warming? No. *Climate change.* Sometimes old words get stuck up here, you know?"

Holland rolled his eyes, making her huff and swat at his arm with her glove. "Yes, because you're *so ancient*, Gamma."

"Tell that to my hair! I've got another white streak comin' in hot, but if the rest of my hair doesn't catch up fast, I can't go on tour as an Emmylou Harris impersonator."

"We'll get Jay to do it, and you can tour as much as you want," Holland replied. "Not the old lady special he does for the coffee house book club. I wouldn't let him do that to you. I swear."

"Your cousin isn't getting *anywhere* near my hair," Gamma shot back. "You are the exceptional Swisher. And you know why."

She was the only one who could get away with such talk, and only around Holland. He didn't have many connections to his mom's family; she'd died when he was little and Gamma had raised him since then. Gamma - Eve Ulrich - had been a mentor to his mom, two women in the architecture field where old boys' clubs still reigned. And when his mom, Daphne, had gone into single motherhood on purpose, she'd earned the ire of her family and Eve's everlasting respect.

From what Gamma had told him over the years, his mom had been a bright thing with a number of demons she'd fought hard for a very long time, but he'd always been the center of her world. And that's how he wound up in Eve's care at the age of four, and since then, she was Gamma. Holland knew he was lucky and loved her with everything he had.

"Jay's really good. Seriously." Holland plopped down in one of the weather-worn wicker chairs that had once been...green, maybe. It was hard to tell after so many wet winters and summers splattered with weeks of brutal sunshine. "I can call him..."

As he expected, Gamma wheeled on him, trowel in hand, and said, "Okay, time for you to get out of my hair," while shooing Holland inside. Holland couldn't stop chuckling at her antics; she'd been saying that line since he was little. Time might have marched on and carried all of them with it, but Gamma was Gamma.

Since she was busy, Holland set about making dinner. Saturday nights were pasta nights, which he usually looked forward to. But as he was standing over the pot, slowly stirring lentil rigatoni, his thoughts kept drifting to the job he'd just accepted. Laurent had been as good as his word and had Holland signing the contract before he left the photo studio, but some part of him felt a little gross about the whole thing. Photographing hot guys for charity? Was that…okay? Was he participating in the fetishization of these guys? But was it fetishization if they'd volunteered for it?

He left Gamma her food in the oven since she wasn't one to "rush pruning". Instead of sitting at their little kitchen table alone, Holland wandered upstairs to give his photo wall another look. He'd left that morning undecided on where to put the photos he'd taken a few weeks ago at a dive bar his friend Jamie had played at with her band, and he was hoping tonight his brain would figure out that particular puzzle piece with nary a second thought.

Holland's bedroom was the converted attic of his Gamma's Cape Cod. It gave him enough privacy and plenty of space to work in, even if it was hot as hell in the summer. And across the northern wall was his continually growing, ever-changing project. From corner to corner, connected by string like a conspiracy theorist's map, were pictures. Some small enough to fit in a locket, others from instant cameras and yet still others made into collages and presented like one image. So many photos documenting the years of his life. Not every moment or every event got a spot on the wall, but if they did, it was because they were special. Memorable. Things that Holland feared, with the graceless slip of time, he'd eventually forget. And he didn't want that.

Truth be told, it scared the shit out of him.

He'd spent his childhood years hoping that some long-lost cousin or half-sibling would pop out of the woodwork, fully formed and eager to love him. It wasn't that he didn't love Gamma. He did. She was his everything. But even as a young kid, Holland had recognized they weren't a "normal" family, and that Gamma was a lot older than most of the parents of his classmates. Time beat a heavier percussion line through his life at an all-too-early age. That same peculiar, but very human, fear was what had driven him to photography.

Little bits of time stamped into paper and saved like they were the most precious mementos. Because they were. What else could conserve a single breath, a single moment, fully formed in all that fraction's color and glory? He'd tried to branch out into video, but those moving images, that tinny laughter, felt hollow to him. Anyone could say anything on a video, do anything on a video, and edit it to show another point of view. A physical photograph didn't have the malleability. And even though he worked primarily in digital for the sake of his job, it was what paid the bills. It didn't *move him* the way a real photograph did.

The wall was his way of keeping time to himself. He'd grown up largely alone. He was used to *alone*. But with the photograph wall, he was anything but *alone*. He was surrounded by *memory*.

Staring at it now while slowly chewing his food, Holland's gaze drifted across the familiar faces, then off the board to the stack of old charity calendars Laurent had given him. He hadn't looked yet and could imagine how *questionable* they were. Charity calendars were for shelter pets and pictures of crowds at community events. Predictable, reliable, great for making people feel bad about Bruce the cat stuck without a home of his own or reminding them of the yearly potato sack race. Charity calendars with people all...well, his mind went scandalous places, like a big burly firefighter gleaming from too much oil and standing behind a conveniently placed cut-out of a snowman.

He'd been right about the shelter animals, at least for the first few examples. They were old, far too old to be useful; the fonts alone reminded him of the gossip rags at the grocery store check-out. A few more were bland but passable, mostly of photos snapped of the previous year's Color Run.

And the last few were exactly what he'd been expecting.

"Well, at least they're not making women pose for these," he said, cringing as he carefully lifted up a page between his index finger and thumb. *Fucking hell.* The one from five years ago didn't pull any punches. These guys were oiled, ripped, and *hot*, and at least half of them were clearly not twenty-something year old twinks. Holland chuckled while he counted them off in his head. *Firefighter, park ranger, mechanic, another firefighter, construction worker, lawyer, plumber...* He kept flipping, noting names that showed up more than once and trying to figure out a way to freshen up the calendar. Last year, the men had posed as Greek gods, and had included trans men and gay couples. It was a good idea, but the over-the-top props made him yearn for something simpler.

"I've got that one," Gamma said from the doorway, two mugs of tea in hand. "My favorite is June. That's Robbie from Radcliffe's Bakery. Owner's son. Nice kid."

Holland peered around the calendar he'd been holding up to raise an eyebrow at her. "You didn't tell me you were a collector."

"Bah. You know you can't make me blush." He got up to take the mug of tea from her and waved her in. "Did you get asked to do this year's calendar?" Gamma asked as she settled in the big armchair by the window, her own cup of tea steaming between her hands.

"Yeah. I guess Laurent is on the Color Run board, and he recommended me, so here I am. Stuck with homework."

Gamma nodded, sipping her tea. "Any ideas percolating up there, kiddo?"

"Not yet. I've got a bit of time before we start."

Holland told her what he knew about the job, concluding with, "And…I don't know. This just feels weird. I'm not gonna make them go rub down with coconut oil beforehand, but apparently these calendars have quite the reputation."

"And you're worried about living up to it all."

He sighed. "I just got a real list of clients going. If I make the calendars good, then Laurent can get me in more doors. Better paying jobs, better paying clients. And I can stop doing weddings except for big ones."

Gamma chuckled at that. "So you can lose all those opportunities to be paid in 'exposure'?"

"Ugh. Don't remind me."

Holland kept flipping through the pages, making notes here and then while she watched and slowly sipped her tea. But the entire time, he could feel her eyes on him. "Anything going on?" Holland asked, hoping he sounded casual despite the knot of worry forming in his stomach.

"Same old, same old. Except…"

Oh god, here it comes. A lump, a tumor, cancer, gangrene, Parkinson's…

"I feel silly about this," Gamma began when Holland finally turned his gaze to her. "But you know how I messed up my back in the spring, trying to move those big pots around?"

"I remember not being happy about it," he said. Truth was, he still felt ashamed for how he'd reacted when Gamma had called from the urgent care clinic. Her friend Josie had driven her over and had assured him she was fine, but he'd raced down there anyways, canceling half a day's worth of jobs to be with the one person who had always been there for him. "I remember trying not to panic."

Gamma put her hand over his and for not the first or even fiftieth time, Holland was struck by how thin her skin looked, the veins dark blue underneath. "Which is why, among other reasons including my back and your sanity, that I hired a gardener. Just to help with the brush and trimming the roses back. You know how out of hand they get."

His Gamma had hired *help*? With her garden? The thing she loved and adored and had since long before he'd come into her life? Holland was stunned, shaking it off long enough to say, "Wait, really? I know we've talked about it before but spring would come around and you wouldn't call anyone, so I figured..." He trailed off. He sounded ridiculous and he knew it. It was just so *surprising*.

The first sign of her acknowledging age. Acknowledging that time did indeed march on the bodies and hearts of all. She was always the strongest person he'd ever known, but a strong spirit wasn't enough to keep a body going. And he'd noticed things - the new glasses with thicker lenses, the extra tubs of arthritis balm in her bathroom when he quietly replaced her towels each morning, the way she'd stand in a room and stare at everything and nothing at the same time.

It still felt like an omission, and he knew how much it took from and of her to admit she needed help. And yet, part of it stung. He'd been so busy with his work over the past few years, but he'd made time to help where he could...right?

Holland flashed back to this past summer and the endless weddings that had helped him buy new equipment and backdrops. A boon to his business for certain. An investment in better opportunities. But that meant more time away from home, and away from her.

Guilt was a nasty thing wedged deep between his ribs, just under his heart. It felt like a knife blade.

"Will you at least let me pay for this gardener?" Holland asked. "Please. I know I haven't been around as much —"

Gamma cut him off with a sharp slash of her hand through the air. A gesture he knew well from a childhood under her roof. It was her *shut up and let me speak, then you can* silent admission. She'd never been harsh with him, not once, but he knew she could be stern. Formidable. "It's my garden, my bill," she said not unkindly. The flint in her eyes spoke loudly enough, anyways. "And Josie recommends him. He starts in two weeks, since we're about to have a frost and that's the right time to start trimming back some things."

Relief. That's what he was feeling now, a wave of it washing over him. Relief that she did this on her own, and that she was acknowledging (however silently) that age catches up to everyone. But that relief was followed by the heat of guilt; an old friend, that one.

"That's great," he managed to say and sound like he meant it. She gave him a small smile but it didn't reach her eyes, so he continued. "No, seriously, Gamma. I mean it. And I'm proud of you."

She rolled her eyes at that. "Don't you start with me, young man."

Holland tried to save face by grimacing, even if it felt strained. "I'm starting nothing, I swear."

"Hmmph."

Holland glanced down at the stack of calendars, following the lines of glistening muscles and too-tight shorts. "Think your gardener wants to pose in a charity calendar?"

That earned him a sharp laugh. "I thought I raised you better!"

"Maybe you just raised me to have good taste?"

Gamma didn't swat at him until she left his room a bit later, but her playfulness didn't help dislodge the lump in his throat. *This sucks.*

Chapter 3

CAIDEN

"Where the hell are you going?"

Richie gave the shovel one last push to get it up under all the other crap in the back of their truck before responding. "I got a thing. And you have a worm on your glove."

Caiden saw the worm, a little thing crawling out of the dirt clod stuck to his glove, and plucked the dirt up to put it back into the garden. "A thing? What thing?"

Richie gave him the eyebrow. "Since when do you care about my comings and goings so much? Nosy."

"I care when you're leaving me high and dry at three in the afternoon on one of our biggest jobs for the fall."

Richie waved him off. "You've more than got it."

Frustration welled in his chest. Richie was great on a job site — funny, quick on his feet, strong as an ox — as long as he didn't have to finish a job. Half-assing was his specialty, especially if it was part of the job he hated, like shoveling fill dirt or cleaning up their gear. He had a green thumb to rival Caiden's but it was like the man rarely wanted to use the muscles rippling under his thin gray t-shirt. That had always been baffling to Caiden but then again...he'd been the one to hire Richie.

"Well, if I'm cleaning up *our* mess," Caiden said as he pushed his shovel's spade deeper into the ground, "then at least tell me what the big secret mission is. This *thing*."

Richie chuckled as he pulled off his hat and wiped dirt from his forehead. It smeared into his sweat and helped make him not look so attractive. Richie was hot. So be it. Caiden wasn't an ass, and he wasn't about to date someone he worked with. "Yeah, all right. Plus, I'll owe you."

Caiden fought back a groan. Richie's version of owing someone meant buying some gas station coffee one morning, not taking the on-call shift on the weekends when some rich asshole's hedges needed trimmed *just so* for a party or whatever rich people did in their ample spare time.

"Got a gig, a modeling thing," Richie said, grinning. "You know, like we talked about."

"You mean when you told me you wanted to do..." Caiden paused, putting the pieces together. When Richie said *modeling*, Caiden had figured for like a local place. But Richie was nearly bouncing with excitement, so unless the man's inner spaniel was amped to eleven, this must have been a bigger thing. *Good for him,* Caiden thought, *but fuck if that grin on his face doesn't make him look like a kid. And I'm officially too old for all this.*

"Yeah, I booked a job! Local charity calendar thing, is what my friend told me. His buddy hooked him up, since they're both firefighters and apparently this calendar was like a big deal forever ago."

Caiden had a very...*inopportune*, sudden memory around those calendars. Specifically swiping them from his mom's desk when she was out of town and trying not to wrinkle the paper under his fingers while he jacked off to Mr. July or Mr. December. His face was hot, he could feel the heat under his skin, but he managed to say,

"Wait, the charity hunks calendar or whatever they were called? I thought those died off ages ago."

Richie shrugged, mountainous shoulders shifting. "Guess they're back then? I don't know, man, I didn't grow up here like you did. But yeah, I guess they're to raise cash for the Color Run and they need models. Monthly models and guys to just pose. Gay couples and trans peeps, too, which is pretty fucking cool."

Richie, you big, loveable idiot. The guy was all bro in the looks department, from the square jaw to the messy surfer-blond hair, but he wasn't a hateful asshole. "Hey, congrats," Caiden said, getting another big grin in return. "They got any room for one more?"

He said it with about half a moment's thought, but the second his question was in the open air, Richie's mouth dropped open. "No, wait, really? Dude! I thought you'd be all against it cause it looks like...I dunno, exploitation or whatever, but it's not! Totally for a good cause! Oh, man, you really want in? The photographer said he was still trying to find people and I think you'd be perfect..."

Caiden turned half an ear to Richie as he pulled out his phone and began texting someone at rapid fire speed; the sight of which only made his own hands cramp.

He'd been half joking.

Right?

Richie held up his phone and Caiden caught the name *Holland Swisher*. It meant nothing to him, but he'd only been back in town a few years. Just long enough to spend that time working nonstop until winter, which took him out to his uncle's cabin until spring thaw hit and the cycle started all over again. "Holland, the photographer, wants to meet. You in?"

This is so stupid. You had to open your big mouth... But the moment Richie had said it was for the Color Run, he knew he was in. The run raised money for kids with cancer, and that was important. It was important to him on a level he couldn't really explain to Richie. It wasn't like he could come out of the gate with, "Oh hey, yeah, I spent my childhood helping to care for my younger sister who lived a lot longer due to money raised to help kids like her". People were too quick to immediately back down, mumble an apology, and then treat him like bruised, ripe fruit. Liable to burst at any second, for any number of reasons.

Reasons he'd cycled through endlessly as a kid. A moody, emo teenager, practically a fixture inside the mall's Hot Topic. An adrift eighteen-year old who went into the Navy, served, and never saw a single gun aimed his way. A late twenty-something who took his brains to a desk every day, and his fears to a gun range every weekend. Then the thirty-something who burned out, cashed in his retirement account, and opened his own landscaping business.

Who now, at forty, was just figuring out who he was. And who he wanted to be; aiming at a dartboard of his own conscience to say *fuck it, what do you have to lose?*

"Yeah, I'm in," Caiden said.

One week later

The note on the glass door said, "If you're here for a calendar shoot, walk around the back to the studio and knock three times."

Caiden stared at the note, written in an elegant hand, and snorted. He'd looked up the photographer, this Holland guy, after agreeing to a day and time via text. He'd noticed right away that Holland never once asked for more than a headshot, so he'd sent over the one on his company's website. Stand, boring professional stuff, with him in a logo ball cap and t-shirt. Not the most flattering thing, but he was pretty sure he wasn't picking up jobs because of his looks. He'd seen that porn video a few times and it never failed to make him laugh at how absurd it was (and didn't that suck, laughing when you were just trying to get your rocks off).

Caiden walked around the side of the brick building, a short strip of shops with the expected dry cleaners, nail place, and tiny coffee shop. The back of the building was mostly run-down loading dock and all the doors were shut tight. It was getting darker out sooner with the oncoming winter, and he could practically feel his mood drag down as the sun sank below the horizon. Seasonal Affective Disorder was a bitch, but he didn't want to botch his shot at this. His sister, Adelaide, had been gone for almost thirty years, and it still felt sometimes like a wound rubbed down with salt.

Don't fuck this up, he thought as he found the photography studio's back door, helpfully labeled with a bright blue note that said: "Delivery? Knock twice. Photography booking, knock three times."

The moment his third knock reverberated against the steel door, his nerves went haywire. People always said he looked so calm all the time, but in reality, he was just really good at disguising the anxiety. Caiden distracted himself by fussing with the straps of his backpack and worried about whether the clothes he brought would be all right or not. The theme was broadly labeled as "heroes", which could mean about anything. And Holland had assured him there were plenty of props and costumes to use, but if he had something he wanted to wear, he could. The main gig was to just pose as yourself with your work, but the photographer had mentioned doing a side project with book heroes, too. Somehow, his Sherlock Holmes cosplay from a literary-themed murder mystery weekend years ago had survived multiple moves and many dented boxes, so Caiden had brought it along just in case.

And staring at the costume had sent him down a rabbit hole of trying to understand how Sherlock Holmes could be sexy…. then he wound up in some rather uh *eye-opening* parts of the internet. Had read things he could never tell anyone about.

(Had maybe bookmarked some of those particular…. stories. Purely for research.)

Caiden didn't realize he was being stared at until he looked up and was met with a pair of hooded eyes on the other side of the door.

"Uh…hi." Caiden smiled, hoping he was being suitably polite to the man who would be photographing him in a rather unsexy costume, then in "varying states of undress, but nothing untoward", as the agreement he'd signed had said. "Holland?"

The door swung open with a squeal of hinges, then Caiden got a good look at Holland the photographer. The man was all angles, from the sharp edges of shoulders and elbows under his plaid shirt, to the long legs encased in black jeans. There'd been no way to tell much about the man's form from a black and white headshot on his website, but standing in front of Holland now, Caiden had never felt so short. He did all right, a little below average, but this guy was like pro-basketball tall.

And he had the blondest hair Caiden had ever seen. Gold-blonde, not white or wheat blonde. Character creator in a video game type of gold. And the dimples…

"Hey, Caiden…right? Caiden Markus." Holland gave him a crooked little grin, which tugged on the scar near his lower lip. It was an old thing, gone almost silvery with age, half-camouflaged by his pale skin, and something about it charmed him. Guy was a photographer, probably spent his days airbrushing corporate or wedding pictures, but he was just a *guy*. Some dude trying to make a living. And scars were just stories written on the body.

The guy in front of him was also killer handsome, but Caiden shoved that aside. He was here to work.

"That's me," Caiden said, hefting his pack a little higher. "I brought the Sherlock costume I mentioned but it's uh…"

Holland didn't even give him a chance to find his words. "Not sexy? Don't worry about it, we can get creative. But we may not need it, so the forward thinking is appreciated." His dark eyes, even darker now that the sun was setting over the building, had a permanently sleepy look to them. They were wide and set far apart and made Caiden just want to stare at this guy. He had a freaking *fascinating*, beautiful face. "Worse comes to worse, you go bare-chested under the cloak and we lean into the whole 'sexy Sherlock" fandom vibe."

Caiden almost choked on his laugh, he was so startled. "Fandom vibe?"

Holland waved a long-fingered hand in the air. "You don't want to know. It's basically porn. Hell, I'm sure there's Sherlock porn out there somewhere. Anyways, come on in…"

Caiden was ushered into a photography studio so clean, he could have licked the floor and tasted wood polish. It was a nice space, with big windows around a ninety-degree angle. The setting sun threw shades of red and orange and purple across the worn floorboards that were covered in old rugs. The photography staging space was just a large white backdrop with a few risers spaced out, but he could see tables beyond that looked stacked with props:

toy swords and capes and helmets, even a pair of angel wings.

"So, figured we'd start with a warm-up. Most people like that, since most people don't have much experience behind a camera," Holland said as he motioned for Caiden to sit on the middle riser. "I'll put your bag over by the table and then we'll walk through this."

Caiden nodded. "You're the boss."

Holland rocked back on his heels, hands stuffed into his pockets, gaze gone contemplative as he looked Caiden up and down. Caiden tried not to squirm under the scrutiny.

"Okay, yeah, this should work," Holland said quietly. Caiden got the feeling he wasn't supposed to hear what Holland was saying, but it would be weird if he stood. Right? Shit. This was already feeling strange in a bunch of different ways, and this was what Caiden had been afraid of. He'd never liked having his picture taken as a kid, especially not the seventh kid in a big family that never had enough time or resources to take care of half of them. He was the middle of the middle, dead center in the sibling line up, and from the time he could remember, pictures always made him feel self-conscious.

But his sister, Adelaide, had loved pictures, so he took them for her. Which meant he could do this for her. He'd never once thought it objectifying or amoral in some way. He just...got fidgety when a camera was out and flashing.

"You need me to do something? Like...I don't know, pose or something?" Caiden asked.

Holland was tapping his thumb against his chin but frowned at Caiden's question. "What? Oh, no, not unless you have some media training you want to put to use. That wasn't snarky, I swear. I was just thinking...could you take off your hat?"

"Shit." Caiden reached up and...yep, he'd left his hat on. "My momma taught me better," he mumbled. "Sorry about that. Stupid of me when I'm here to get pictures taken." Tugging the elastic out of his hair took a moment longer.

But Holland was now grinning at him and nodding. It made those wide, dark eyes flash in a way that absolutely didn't make his stomach flip. "I knew it. I knew there was good hair under that hat. You probably wear them all the time for work, so it was nothing to slip on on your way out the door. Habit."

Caiden's brain and mouth went out of sync for a long moment. "You knew my hair was good? What if I was bald?"

He shrugged, turning all those angles and edges into something softer. "Then we would have gone with it. But the photo on your company's website? There's a bit of hair poking out from the bottom of your cap. So, I figured it was fifty-fifty. And that," Holland said, pointing to Caiden's head, "is even better. I love photographing blue hair. It really shows up on camera."

"Really?" Caiden resisted the urge to touch the blue streaks in his brown, wavy hair. He'd recently started doing them again and spent several minutes after each fresh dye job contemplating if he was too old to do such things. His love of the blue won out every time, but they were narrow victories.

"Yeah. And I've already got some good ideas for how it works with your Sherlock Holmes costume."

Caiden grinned. This guy was an odd mix of hyper and intelligent and it was fun to see what would come out of his mouth next. And that was pure bait to old flirting instincts, ones that rose to the surface like little bubbles. "Sherlock cloak with the bare chest, huh?"

"Do you have a partner who would like to be photographed? I

have a great idea but it really only works with two people."

This guy's mind must be a maze, Caiden thought as he watched Holland back up to eye the space better. "Yeah, no can do. Sorry."

"No....to the partner who wants to be photographed?"

Caiden shook his head. "No to the partner. Bit of a loner."

"No worries. We've got plenty to work with." Holland slipped behind his photography rig, an elaborate thing that looked expensive as hell, and said, "Hey, Caiden?"

"Yeah?"

"Smile for me."

Caiden smiled. Holland snapped the picture, then two more in rapid succession, and immediately went to a pair of monitors. Caiden's heart got stuck in his throat for a moment, his worst childhood fears pushing against his muscles, but then Holland said, "Perfect", and his world righted.

I can do this, he thought as Holland came back to him. "Want to see?"

"Yeah. I do."

Chapter 4

CAIDEN

Caiden steeled himself. He didn't *hate* pictures of himself but was happy to blend into the background. Hard to do when he was usually shuffled into the front row of group photos, his height a disadvantage in all those little ways that made life as a short man difficult. Annoying, most of the time, but you try dating other guys and nonbinary folks when almost every single one of them was taller. Eventually, someone made a remark. And in the dating days of his more recent past, it was *always* mentioned. It wasn't worth the hassle anymore. People were so damn oblivious to how hurtful their words could be.

Standing beside Holland now, as they leaned in to look at a laptop monitor, Caiden didn't feel that strange shadow. The one that every tall person cast over him that felt, well…diminutive in some way. Holland wasn't doing that strange lean-in some folks did, and he wasn't moving the monitor down toward him.

It felt a little like Holland didn't even notice. And now that he was thinking about it, Caiden hadn't once felt cowed while they'd talked, or when Holland had taken the photos. He'd just done it. Professional, smooth, easy.

The picture on the monitor in front of them was good. Shockingly good. "I can add in backgrounds or whatnot if you want.

Some people like the clean emptiness of the white, though. Whatever your preference is."

Caiden glanced up at him, confused. "I thought this was just a test photo, to make sure I didn't panic or whatever."

"It is. But it's also *your* picture." Holland moved his finger over the laptop trackpad, zooming in until it looked like a headshot. "I'm just the photographer, but in my professional opinion, this is a good one to hang onto. You never know."

It was hard not to fidget a little. He was the sole focus of this stranger's assessing gaze and it felt...*weird*. Though that word didn't give full credence to how odd this all was. Caiden was used to working in the background - one of four or five or ten people covered in dirt and sweating, doing their jobs and doing them well. You dig, plant, mulch, mow, and hack, hand the client the invoice, and that's it. On to the next job.

Holland's job wasn't that. Far from it. It was weird, and a little flattering. Just a little. If he thought about it too much, he'd start shrinking back into the shadows. Caiden looked around, anxious to change the subject, and took five steps over to a box overflowing with stuff on a nearby table. "Hope you don't have any down in here, I'm allergic," he said, pointing to a clump of neon-hued feathers.

Holland froze, eyes narrowed, then his lean frame sagged. "Oh, no, that's for the cats." He came over to pull the feathers out, which turned into some kind of toy on the end of a long stick. "I photograph a lot of cats. You'd think it would be dog people who go nuts over having their photos taken, but cat people are a whole different breed."

"Different species, too."

Holland chuckled. "And that."

Caiden picked up the toy and wiggled it around, making the bell on the end jangle. "So cat people are at the top of the list of uh...demanding clients?"

"Oh, no. That would be bird people."

"No shit?"

"Truly." Then Holland smiled at him. "Want to see? I just took pictures of a guy with his bird. Who was wearing an eyepatch."

Two minutes later, Caiden was looking at a picture of a very regal scarlet macaw, with an eyepatch, resting on the shoulders of a man who could have made a killing at cosplaying a pirate. "Okay, I love everything about this," Caiden said as he leaned in. "You got the lighting just right, cause it's glinting but not bouncing off the buttons on the guy's vest. And the whole thing looks...I don't know the word for it. Warm? The colors of the velvet of his pants and the...satin? I think it's satin around his waist. And the bird is a focus, but it's not overshadowing the human subject." He pulled away to find Holland staring at him. "Sorry."

"Don't apologize." If anything, Holland sounded a little stunned. He worked his jaw back and forth a few times, but that only drew Caiden's eye to the pink rising high on his cheeks. From this angle, half a head shorter than Holland, it was a good view.

Caiden stepped back and Holland closed out the photo, leaving the sparse logo of his company on the screen. He almost asked to see the photo again. This guy had a gift. "I've always liked photography. Spent many a summer reading my Nan's old *National Geographics* and jotting down the photographer's names so I could look them up at the library."

God, shut up, Caiden. You're doing that thing where you scare off a total stranger with your nonsense.

"I feel like I should apologize, standing here gaping like I am."

When Holland came near this time, he brought with him a scent; one that went straight to Caiden's gut. Crisp and fresh, a little bit like some of those department store colognes, but less *cosmetic* and more natural. Something that sat close to the skin.

Caiden almost stepped back, just to get some air, when Holland continued. "I see a lot of people through any week, but few of them actually like photography the way you do. They pay for a service and they get it. Sometimes I get some gushing, but to be honest, most people are a little selfish, so they gush over themselves in the photo. I take it as the mark of a job well done. Every now and then, someone will say something about the backdrop or the lighting, and that's a moment of pride. But you're...maybe the first to really *notice.*"

Holland suddenly laughed and swiped a hand over his face. Whatever was slowly weaving itself between them, some kind of insta-flirtation or flicker of attraction, was pulled taut. Then snapped. "I sound like a lonely, maudlin artist. That was not professional of me. Suffice to say, I appreciate your kind words and attention to detail. And I'm glad you like your test photograph. If you're okay to proceed, we should book a time for our first session. It's the same for everyone unless they have an objection: a set of photos based around your occupation."

Caiden took a moment to let his mind settle. Something had definitely come to life between them, but Holland had been the one to pull it back. He had to respect that. They were here to do a job, after all, and he didn't need to get distracted while trying to pose shirtless or in some state of undress. *Remember what — and who — you're doing this for.*

"Yeah, all good. So, do you want me to bring a shovel or something with me?"

Holland nodded. "Yeah, a shovel if you've got one you can spare. Even better if it looks like it's actually been used. We'll do some shots inside, on a backdrop, and if the weather holds that day, we can go to the little patch of woods behind the studio. Nothing risqué, some tight t-shirt pictures and some shirtless ones, and then we can plan what you want to do next."

Caiden perked up at that. "I thought there was like a theme or something. For the calendar."

Holland smiled at him. "There is. It's about showing bodies, and humans, in all their shapes and sizes. I went through all the calendars from the past and the superheroes and Greek gods and the "sexy firefighter" stuff is all fine and good, but I want to inspire people with this calendar. If we inspire, more people buy it, and the more money goes to the charity. So we're showing people in action. Work, life, sports, love. Honestly, the 'heroes' theme was just to get people in the door, but we'll still do it. I'll need extra material for stretch goals if the fundraiser goes well."

Caiden couldn't stop the smile spreading across his face. Holland was so damn *passionate* as he talked about his vision, and it made him light up. The kind of glow that only real, deep love caused, and it made everything about Holland golden.

Ah, shit, Caiden thought as Holland discussed next steps and pulled out an old-school planner to help them find a date and time for their session. *I've got a crush.*

Caiden didn't live alone by choice. Richie had bunked with him for about six months, before an apartment in a complex near his parents had opened up. Before that, he'd played host to several renters; some good, some not so much. And every time he found himself suddenly alone in a three-bedroom apartment he only had because of his father passing, Caiden started missing the noise. Even a shitty roommate was still a roommate, and that meant three am flushing toilets and dropped silverware and the creak of the refrigerator door hinge or squeal of that one floor plank.

Living alone meant silence.

When that silence greeted him after he returned from Holland's studio, Caiden pulled out a record at random and put it on the turntable. He didn't have the thing because the sound was "warmer" or whatever audiophile bullshit was spewed online; it had been his dad's, and his dad had been his best friend, so keeping it meant keeping a little bit of his dad close by.

The airy sounds of light jazz permeated the silence, and Caiden was finally able to relax. He could finally let his body unwind enough to go scrounge in the kitchen until his stomach caught up with his mind.

And if he was cooking and moving around, then it wasn't silent. And he wouldn't get stuck thinking about Holland. A total stranger. A super nice guy who was wickedly talented. A guy who was very much Caiden's type — tall, blonde, lanky. Oh, he'd date almost anyone out the gate, gave everyone a chance. But it was no coincidence past long-term partners (count of two) had been the same physical type.

Caiden cracked a few eggs into a skillet and began adding spices. He was halfway through the third rotation on the pepper grinder when he caught himself thinking about Holland's dark eyes. And his goddamn fascinating face. "Jesus Christ," he muttered, setting the pepper grinder aside so hard it toppled. "Fuck, stop it. You're not helping yourself."

So, he had a crush. Fine.

Fine.

2 hours later

Caiden was not fine. After scrolling through every streaming service he had, checking the movies to rent, and then going through his DVD library, he wound up in bed, laptop off to the side, with a hand wrapped around his cock while on the screen two very attractive men sucked each other off.

It had started as boredom, but the moment he'd gotten *invested* in the happenings on the screen, he'd let his eyes drift shut. And swimming to the surface of his consciousness was not the face of that square-jawed superhero movie star or the muscles of that guy on that one show about hackers...of course not. It had been Caiden's face and that was *not* okay. Fantasizing about movie stars or celebrities was fine, most people did that. But he was not going to fantasize about a real person he needed to face at least two or three more times. It felt beyond weird, almost intrusive and demeaning.

So, he kept his eyes, and his focus, on the screen. The pair in the video had swapped off to some light fingering and the one getting said treatment was panting enticingly. Okay, good, this was good.

No, really, it was just a way for him to get his rocks off and go to bed, but at least he was paying attention.

The man doing the fingering was whispering filth and Caiden's ears perked up at that. He'd never used to think dirty talk did it for him, but you learn a lot about yourself in your late thirties, especially if you're newly single and your friends take you out cruising.

"Right there," the man getting fingered gasped. "Oh, fuck." He actually looked like he was having a good time; when he gripped the sheets, the veins in his considerable forearms stood out and his ruddy complexion reddened even more.

Something twisted low in Caiden's gut and he groaned. He was starting to leak a little, so he spread the wetness around, added more lube, and kept watching. There were now three fingers involved and a lot of creative cursing, which was great, but the moment they started to kiss was even hotter. Three fingers deep, the guy on top (who was all sinewy muscle and tattoos and olive skin a few shades deeper than his own) was skillfully tongue-fucking his partner's mouth in time with fucking his ass.

Caiden could only dig his heels into the mattress and groan. He needed *more*. This was so good, but he'd always been a bit slow to get going, and the sounds of lips and tongues meeting and their moaning wasn't *enough*. And his silicone plug was all the way across the room, nestled in its little bag in his top dresser drawer.

"Come on," Caiden grunted, half aggravated, half aroused. He looked over at the screen to see they'd moved on — still kissing and then....oh. Guy on top was kissing his way down the other guy's ample chest, sucking on his nipples and making his partner's voice jump half an octave. Caiden reached up to pull at his own nipple, watched it go taut, then bounce back. His were only sensitive when he was turned on, but once he told a partner that, they usually made it their mission to get him to that point. (A lot of the guys he'd slept with enjoyed that, and he got something out of it, too, so who was he to stop them?)

"Turn over, baby."

Caiden narrowed his eyes but kept watching. The pair shifted around, taking time to messily make out, and a moment later, the bottom was ass-up and his partner was practically nibbling on his cheeks.

"Oh, fuck. Fuck, right there -"

There was no stopping it. The moment his eyes were shut, Caiden let his free hand drift down, until he was running a finger over his perineum and shuddering.

"Fuck. Fuck. Your tongue....shit, babe, god!"

Caiden managed to see two seconds of enthusiastic ass-eating, the kind where there were finger indents left in hips and the guy feasting was covered in slobber from eyes to chin.

"Fuck, yeah, right there, right there! Fuck it feels like you're *in me...*"

Caiden groaned. This hard, this turned on, he could image a firm, warm tongue licking a broad stripe right where he needed it. The press of thick muscle against his hole. Pushing, pressing, circling, over and over until Caiden was reaching back to spread himself, to create more space for the brilliant tongue fucking him out of his mind.

"Oh god. Yes, *please,*" Caiden said. The room was empty, but his head was full of a mystery lover who did everything exactly *right.* "Put it in me, put it in me..."

"I'm gonna fuck you until you're crying for it," the top on screen snarled, making his partner whine and shove back. "And when you come, I'm going to keep fucking you."

"Fuck, fuck, fuck," Caiden chanted, now so caught up in everything that whatever they were doing on the screen didn't matter. He was horny and almost there. He pressed one finger against his hole, felt it spasm under the pressure, and right as he stroked down with a tight fist, he pushed his finger inside.

He came hard enough that his ears were ringing with it, his body singing. Alive. He felt *alive*.

And ten seconds later, when the first highs of coming his brains out wore off, he realized he was a fucking mess. He felt great, and he was exhausted. And maybe now he could get over his little crush and move on.

Chapter 5

HOLLAND

"Damn."

Holland stepped back from his photo wall and rubbed his eyes. He'd been staring at it all night, but his brain wasn't interested in the routine. It was supposed to go "stare at the board, find the empty spots, fill imagination with possibilities" until he couldn't hardly stand up straight from exhaustion. Some people had bedtime routines, he had one on which the distant goal of sleep was hung up and left to swing in the wind. Holland wasn't a fan of the term "insomniac", especially since a lot of people used it colloquially like they said "OCD" and "allergic"; several stones' throws away from the medical terminology. What they meant was "tired", "stressed", and "I don't like it". "Insomniac" felt wrong to him. How did one describe years of interrupted sleep for no reason at all? The doctors didn't have an answer, and every therapist he'd been to had told him to try different things.

White noise.

Herbal tea before bed.

Meditation.

Counting sheep. (*Seriously.*)

None of it made any difference. But the photo wall was soothing, at least, and he could count on that. Most of the time. Tonight was not one of those, apparently.

It was after two a.m. and the best he'd do tonight would be a few hours, maybe a nap on the office couch between sessions in the studio. Holland sank down on his bed and buried his hands in his hair.

I should get a haircut. It's so long.

Well, he did have scissors in the bathroom. Why wait? He could cut his own hair. He was an artist —

Holland groaned. When his sleep was this disrupted, his mind went to bonkers places. No, of course he wasn't going to give himself a middle of the night haircut. That was foolish, and he'd look ridiculous.

But the urge to do something...*anything*...was gnawing at him.

After a few minutes of fussing with the pillows and pulling out his laptop, Holland opened his photo gallery. The last few days had mostly been shooting people interested in doing the calendar. Well, *calendars* now, since the interest had been so surprisingly high. And everything he'd done so far had been basic stuff: simple poses and headshots, a few seated figures. A couple of people had been insistent they get to wear their hero outfit. Holland was still recovering from that, especially since there had somehow been two people who wanted to be shirtless Edmond Dantes. It fit, kind of, but without the proper staging, Holland hadn't been able to really capture the dashing hero vibes.

He kept flipping, pausing on a few photos that he put into a folder of strong contenders. A fifty-something tattooed fireman. A nonbinary couple in their thirties. One guy who was so classically handsome, he reminded Holland of the boxers from the 1940s and 50s.

When he got to the last set of pictures, Holland couldn't help but pause. It had been two days since Caiden had come into his studio, and he hadn't looked at the images since. But he'd known immediately that this guy had something. He had a round, open face and an easy smile, but it was some unnamed thing that had gotten snared in Holland's little mind trap. Stuff got stuck in there all the time; it was part of the allure and annoyance of being a photographer. (He'd once told a date that he just saw the world differently and apparently that had come off snobbish. Somehow. There hadn't been a second glass of wine, let alone a second date with that one.)

And Caiden had made the cut. Poor guy. Now all Holland had to do was not act ridiculous around him when Caiden stopped by for the first real shoot at the end of the week and it would be fine. Because he'd have figured out *what* it was about this guy that had snagged his attention. He wasn't loud, wasn't egotistical, didn't think he was better than everyone else. He'd been practically *shy* when Holland had suggested doing headshots first.

Oh. Holland realized he'd stepped back from the board and he'd been staring glassy-eyed at the right side of it while Caiden's smile and the way he'd smelled like fallen leaves were glued to his gray matter. The photographs on this side of the board were from nearly a decade ago, when he'd decided to start photographing events in the evenings and on weekends. His job as a technical writer had lacked any creativity or nuance, which he'd known was part of the gig. But it left him itching after every day of mindless hours in an office where the lights were too yellow and the carpet smelled like wet dog.

He peered over the faces from all those years ago. His college roommates had scattered to the four winds after graduation, but for the first few years, they tried to meet up for a week somewhere.

By the time he'd started his photography business, those few years had been all it took to pull them apart. People got married, had kids, got divorced, changed jobs two, three, eight times like true Millennials. When he thought about that time that had been so pivotal in figuring out who he was — as a gay man, an artist, his own person outside of Gamma's life — and some part of him missed that. He didn't miss the stress, didn't miss the shitty food and dingy clubs, but he missed having someone to talk to like they would, until three in the morning on the frigid cast iron patio furniture and hacking from gas station cigars, stumbling through the dorm's back door before one of the RAs found them.

That's who Caiden had instantly reminded him of. An easy-going nature that didn't take itself too seriously. And on a deeply selfish level, someone who had seen and recognized his skill with an artist's soul. Caiden had been complimentary, yes, but the passion in his voice had instantly caught his attention. He just...seemed like someone he should get to know.

And until he could figure out a way to not be weird about it, he'd remain professional. No one except Gamma would ever call him charming, but he could be friendly. Easy to work with. Maybe even fun enough to make Caiden want to hang out after a shoot?

Holland shut his laptop, slid it onto the nightstand, and hit the lamp switch. Letting his thoughts jumble up and release was sometimes exactly what he needed in order to be able to sleep. He just hoped he didn't dream of better times and never be able to find that joy again.

Caiden's text read: "Sorry, running ten minutes behind", followed by a thumb's down.

Holland chuckled as he quickly typed out a reply. "No worries, you're my last appointment of the day. Don't rush on my account." And he meant it. The first days of shooting for the calendar had gone pretty smoothly, so all the nerves he usually felt at the beginning of a new project had slowed to a simmer.

And, truthfully, being surrounded by photography subjects who were volunteering their time for a good cause? It made him feel less gross about the whole exploitation thing that had given him pause to begin with. Everyone had been good-natured and friendly, if not downright kind. No arguments about poses. He heard their suggestions and they heard his. The work was *good*. The photos were...well...damn near the best stuff he'd ever shot.

He looked over at Freddie and Sam, a nonbinary couple dressed as pirates right out of Robert Louis Stevenson, who were taking a handful of selfies now that their session was done. They were cute together, and Holland had seen the way they'd looked at each other. Star-crossed and sweet, all at the same time. The artfully ripped costumes showed plenty of skin. Sexy but sophisticated.

So no, Holland didn't mind the extra few minutes to swap out the set. A few extra minutes to get his head on straight before his not-crush *crush* would arrive and probably throw him for a loop again. He'd play it cool — he had to — but a bit more time to calm the butterflies was good.

Freddie and Sam ducked into the back room to change, then

Holland handed them the QR code card where they could view the whole gallery of photos once he got the editing done. Once they left, he started moving set pieces around for Caiden's session. The wide garage door at the back of the studio was flung open, the smell of a late autumn afternoon immediately floated in.

"Uh, hey? Sorry, the back door was open —"

Holland shot up straight from his deep hunch over his laptop at the sound of Caiden's voice. "Hey, yeah no worries."

And then he got a look at Caiden.

"Oh."

Shit.

It had been well over a week since they'd met. Caiden had been smooth-faced then, but he was now sporting a seriously sexy, deep brown five o'clock shadow that was doing *something* to Holland's insides. And that it was paired with a white t-shirt so tight, he could see the barbells through Caiden's nipples…well, he was absolutely staring. Guilty as sin.

Caiden smiled at him. "Oh? Something wrong?"

The question sounded innocent, but he heard the amusement buried beneath.

Shit, how obvious am I being right now? Holland jerked his gaze away, waving a hand at the open door instead. "Figured we'd do some shots outside, since the weather's decent." He glanced over at Caiden again, then looked away. "If you don't mind being outside in the wind."

"Doesn't bother me." Caiden walked over and set his backpack down on the empty side table and propped a shovel up against the bag. "I'm used to working outside. Landscaper and all that."

"Right. Of course." *Holland, you idiot. You sound ridiculous right now.* "Uh, yeah, anyways….do you need to change?"

Caiden looked down at himself, hands at his sides. "Is there a stain or something? I thought this was all clean when I changed at work but —"

Holland nearly smacked his own forehead. "No, no, you're fine. I'm being stupid. Landscaper, right. Of course. Of course."

Stop rambling. You idiot.

He blew out a breath, then tucked himself in behind the camera, wishing for walls and a ceiling so he could be embarrassed in private. No such luck, and all he could do was hope his cheeks weren't as red as they felt, and if they were, that Caiden didn't notice.

Caiden, though, was chuckling and not unkindly. "I can imagine you have all the lines you run through at every appointment memorized. I get it. Same with us, all that customer service talk."

Holland had to laugh at that. "Am I that obvious? I *have* been here all day, but I promise it won't affect the photos."

Caiden eyed the simple chair-on-a-backdrop set with raised eyebrows. "Scandalous set for our first photoshoot. A chair. My goodness."

"Okay, okay. Well, clearly I did something right last time, since you came back and you're already making fun of me."

Caiden's pretty lips twitched. The movement made a scar on his jaw ripple and, looking up, Holland realized Caiden had a tiny heart tattooed inside the upper cartilage of his ear. He almost asked about it, but shrugged the thought away. *Professional. Remember. Be professional.* "Let's start with some seated ones, like last time, then we can bring in the shovel."

"And take off my shirt?" Caiden's stare was a little too warm. Like he was daring Holland to respond in a certain way, which only made Holland confused. This was a job, not an excuse to flirt on paid time. It was fine if Caiden did it, but he shouldn't engage.

Holland adjusted the lenses as Caiden sat very straight-backed in the chair, head held high with an easy, friendly smile. The warmth in his eyes felt a little more than friendly, though. "If you want. It's not required. I figured we'd use the patch of woods out back for a couple of shots. Maybe of you digging and wiping your forehead."

"Dirt is sexy?"

He bit back another laugh. "Hey, to each their own. A little dirt rarely hurts anyone."

Holland clicked the final lens in place and Caiden came fully into focus. He got a few shots in before Caiden asked, "What about you?"

That smile, that tone, and that damn five o'clock shadow were slowly killing him and they weren't even really rolling yet. "What about me? And, how about we switch it up?"

Caiden let his posture soften and he shifted positions easily, going from both feet on the floor to one leg crossed ankle to knee. He clasped his hands around the knee on top and tilted his head. Holland stared for a moment. This guy was a natural, somehow, and it was helping him feel less...stiff, professionally speaking.

"How's that?"

"Perfect." Holland took more pictures, then had Caiden shift once more. He opted to lean back in the chair and put his hands behind his head. Chest puffed out, hips tilted up a little.

Those damn nipple piercings pressed so tightly against his thin, white t-shirt.

And his arms...fuck, just *lines* of muscle pressed against olive skin.

Caiden stared at the camera. Holland stared at him.

"So...do you like things a little dirty, sometimes?" Caiden

grinned and Holland snapped that so fast, he could have broken the button. "Professionally speaking. I major in dirt every day. So, what's photography's version of dirty?"

"Food fight at a wedding." He didn't even have to think about it. It took him months before he shot footage at another wedding, and even then, he'd doubled his retainer.

Caiden stared at him for a moment, then laughed so sharply, the sound echoed in the wide-open space. "No shit?"

Okay, good. This is good. A story I can do. "Yeah. Apparently it was planned but no one thought to tell me. I only figured it out when someone smashed cake on my head." He suppressed a slight smile at the memory. "It wasn't all horrible, since I did get to throw cake at the person who got me. They weren't thrilled."

"A little reciprocity never hurt." Whether he meant to or not, Caiden flexed his shoulders, as if he made to roll them and aborted halfway through, and all Holland could see were muscles and nipple rings. He felt dizzy.

"Want to see these before we move outside?" he managed to ask.

"Let's do it."

Caiden was a spry thing, all lean muscle but broad in the chest and shoulders, and he was *warm*. All of this hit Holland at once as Caiden leaned around him to take a look. The desk housing the computer and monitors wasn't huge, but two people could stand in front of it comfortably.

If Caiden was a little closer than appropriate for acquaintance-status, Holland was having a hard time seeing it as anything but purposeful.

"Wow, yeah, okay.... huh." Caiden cocked his head and examined the image grid, then motioned for Holland to enlarge one. "Maybe this is your version of dirty. Getting us camera-shy people to talk. Open up. Relax." He pointed at his face. "I always look pinched in pictures. But not here."

"Agreed." It was all Holland could manage to say. Because Caiden was close and warm (he did mention warm, right?) and smelled like laundry detergent, sunshine, and earth.

"You some kind of magician?"

"Not in the least."

"Think I'd have to argue with that one." Caiden shifted, turning to prop a hip on the desk and stare up at Holland with his hands in his pockets. "Pretty sure you're a magician. I don't look like an antisocial asshole in these pictures, and I am *extremely* self-effacing when it comes to seeing myself on camera. So clearly, that means you're a magician."

Caiden had no poker face. At all. The guy was grinning ear to ear and clearly trying to yank Holland's chain. Okay, fine. He could play that way. "Well, then this magician insists that his current audience participation member head outside so we can get some action shots from the antisocial asshole landscaper."

Caiden threw him a little salute. "Ay, ay, boss."

"That's magician boss to you."

Caiden cracked open a laugh and marched through the studio, stopping only to snag his backpack with one hand. "You got somewhere I can change?"

"Down the hall, bathroom is on the left."

Caiden disappeared and it took everything Holland had to not collapse in relief on his desk. That man was *trouble*, and he wasn't sure if he could talk himself out of playing along.

Chapter 6

CAIDEN

The giddy sensation in his stomach wasn't nerves. Not anymore. It had quickly morphed into that same roller coaster thrill that meeting someone new and interesting provided, and it had been a damn long time since Caiden had felt that.

Okay, yes, he was nervous. A little. But it was *exciting*, not anxiety-inducing. He could already see Holland taking a mallet to his own shell; being willing to play along and tease back. This guy was *fun* once you got past the stoic professionalism.

(Holland being tall and blonde and gorgeous helped, too.)

Caiden threw on the muscle tank that was only a few shades darker than the blue streaks in his hair, then swapped his nice, clean, *professional* jeans out for ones that were much tighter and sat low on his hips. The damn things were ages old, from a time when it seemed like everyone wore their jeans below their hip bones and were all one sneeze away from bursting the seams.

But after a few moments of studying himself in the mirror, he wasn't sure. He'd brought other options. Maybe he needed a second opinion. It didn't take long for Caiden to conjure up the image of a Holland slightly slack-jawed and dark-eyed at his uh...*choice* of apparel. He just hoped he wasn't pushing too hard, too fast. That had been the downfall of many a budding relationship, and even after a handful of hours in Holland's presence, Caiden knew he liked the guy. And he wanted to know more. But he didn't want to be *too* obvious. The flirting was fun. Easy. No pressure. And honestly, he was too old for drawn-out games.

"Hey, Holland?" Caiden asked, voice raised as he peered around the bathroom door.

"Yeah?"

Caiden managed to keep a straight face as he replied. "So I don't know which pair of pants to wear. And I feel ridiculous in these other jeans I brought."

There was a moment of silence, then footsteps, then a knock at the door. "You brought other options?"

For the first time since he'd arrived, Caiden felt a flush of embarrassment. When he'd packed clothing options for the shoot, he thought *maybe* he could slip in some gentle flirting or teasing. Get Holland's cheeks to turn pink. All in good fun. But doubt was a monster, and now he was feeling some kind of other way about all of this.

"Yeah, I did. But maybe I should just wear the jeans I had on already?" As he said it, he was stuffing his clothes into his backpack. "I'm guessing you don't want the pictures to be *too much*."

Another beat of silence, one that rang in Caiden's head. "Do you need a professional opinion?"

Holland had thrown him a lifeline and Caiden grasped at it. "Yeah, that'd be great, actually."

Holland poked his head in, took one look at Caiden in his muscle shirt and tight, *tight* jeans, and audibly swallowed. Okay, that was…. unexpected but not unwelcome. Caiden focused on standing very still and letting Holland look him over.

Professional. Totally.

Holland eventually looked away and yep, there was a bit of blushing going on and goddamn if it wasn't cute as hell. "Haven't seen hip huggers since 2002," he said with a small chuckle. "Are you comfortable in them?"

The need to move, to squirm in some way, had Caiden shifting from foot to foot. "I mean, they suck to wear, but I could handle it for some pictures."

To Caiden's surprise, Holland came into the bathroom and held out his hand. "You said you have other options. Can I see them?"

"Yeah, sure." Caiden pulled out the jeans he'd walked in wearing, along with some running tights, a pair of black, tailored slacks (totally part of a suit he owned for weddings and funerals), and a pair of tight, but not obscene, athletic shorts that reached mid-thigh.

"These ones." Holland held the shorts out to him. "If you're okay in them."

"Quick decision-making," Caiden said as he took the shorts. "And yeah, they're better than the jeans by a mile."

That earned him a grin. "It's for purely selfish reasons."

Holland made to leave but stopped when Caiden said, "Sharing is caring, you know."

When Holland turned to face him, he was wearing a rather serious expression and Caiden's stomach dropped. *Oh shit. I went too far. Shit shit shit.* "Professionally speaking," Holland said as he stepped closer, "the shorts add a nice variety. I haven't had anyone wear shorts for their sexier shoot yet, and you've got the physique for them. I'm sure spending all day shoveling and pruning and weeding is like working out for eight to ten hours."

It was like a punch to the gut, wrapped in the softest silk. Caiden wasn't an egotistical man by any means, but he was proud of his hard work day in and day out. And that hard work had helped him stay fit after struggling with his weight as a teenager. His parents had been good people, but their understanding of health and wellness had been sorely lacking, and the occasional lack of money for fresh food had made it even more difficult. When you were hungry, calories were calories, no matter how empty.

"Something like that."

Then Holland stepped back and the air rushed into the room, leaving Caiden blinking and gripping the shorts a little tighter than necessary. "Come out when you're ready," Holland said over his shoulder as he made to leave. "Oh, and it's just a thought but would you be okay taking your hair down? Not to start, but for the last few sets."

Caiden ran his fingers across his undercut; it was visible with his hair pulled up and the sharp rasp against his skin made something in his spine shudder. "Sure."

The smile Holland shot him was wide and pleased and it made Caiden want to see it again, but in different circumstances. Maybe across a table at a restaurant or while side by side on a hike. *Or in my bed.*

The door clicked shut and Caiden didn't waste time changing, then walked back behind the strip mall to the patch of scraggly woods and overgrown weeds, shovel in hand. Holland was doing the requisite camera-fussing, so Caiden made sure to speak up on approach. "Where do you want me?"

Holland motioned to a simple wood chair. "Seated, then standing. Maybe leaning on the shovel. Then...well, if you want to get creative, by all means."

Holland's lips did this cute little twitch thing that begged to be egged on. Caiden grinned. "Ooo, creative license, I like it. I'm guessing maybe show a little leg, some chest?"

Holland's eyes shot to his chest and Caiden's suspicion was confirmed. This guy maybe had a thing for piercings, the way he kept looking at Caiden's with those heavily-hooded eyes and ever so slight lift of his eyebrows. It was a sexy, come-hither thing Caiden was really coming to enjoy.

Flirting was fun. Teasing was even better.

"I'm thinking maybe like this." Caiden lifted the hem of his muscle shirt as if to wipe sweat from his brow and thrust out his chest a little, with his other hand firmly clamped around the shovel's handle. He carried through the motion, then let the shirt drop. "What do you think? All sweaty and glistening? That enough titillation for the camera?"

It sure looked like Holland's grip on his camera had tightened, the way the skin at his knuckles had gone bone white. Caiden had to bite the inside of his cheek to keep from grinning. "I think that unless you want to work up a sweat digging a hole for no reason, we'll need to get you wet."

Silence

Silence

Several seconds of them staring each other down, Holland's deep, wide, dark gaze twisting him up inside.

Caiden couldn't take it any longer and burst out laughing. "Holy shit, you said that with the most serious expression and I *can't...*" He trailed off when Holland started to laugh as well and the tension between them burst. "Get me wet, huh?"

Holland's grin was a thing of beauty. "I have a spray bottle in the back."

"I've got a hose in my truck."

"Tempting," Holland replied as he grew pink in the cheeks and looked adorable, "but there's no hookup out here. We'd need more space and somewhere that was okay to spray down. Don't think the property owners would love us making mud back here." But he looked away, gaze rolled skyward in thought. "If you're serious, I bet we could use my Gamma's house. She's got a nice backyard and a bit of a decline in the back, where runoff wouldn't be a problem."

"I'm absolutely down. And we should use a kiddie pool," Caiden said. "That would work, right?"

"Yeah, I think so."

Feeling all kinds of satisfied with himself, Caiden took a couple of steps toward the chair, putting him close enough to put one booted foot up on it. "Then maybe we should get to the photos today so we can plan for this special shoot."

"Special shoot? Your words, not mine."

Bastard was teasing him. The tone was dead dry, but Holland clearly was a smiley guy and that adorable little twitch near the dimple in his left cheek was the giveaway. *Cute as could be*, he thought before replying. "Making an appointment specifically to spray me down, and at your relative's house? Don't keep spoiling me, I might just stick around."

Holland didn't reply to that, but as he leaned down to press his eye to the camera, he tossed Caiden a wink.

Holland didn't send over the address to his relative's place until the morning they were to meet, and Caiden immediately realized it looked familiar. He'd been doing more initial walkthroughs and estimates lately, but he'd also been training a new guy on staff, so he'd been riding shotgun for a couple of weeks. He recognized it was on the east side of town, where most of the neighborhoods were Cape Cods and brick ranch houses, but it wasn't until he threw his car into park in front of the perfect white picket fence that he fully recognized the place.

Moreover, he recognized the sprightly older woman who was walking up the path with a surprised smile on her face. He and Richie and the new guy, Sven, had just dug out half a dozen withered rose bushes to be replaced with something else in the spring. He'd left Richie and Sven to do the afternoon work at the house, but he remembered the client, Eve. Funny, whip smart, and the kind of woman who reminded him of his mother and grandmother: the kind that took no sass but never held back on affection.

Eve was waving him down as Caiden got out of his car. "Don't tell me *you're* the gardener Holland is shooting this morning," she said.

Caiden could only laugh at the coincidence. Of *course* this would happen. "I mean, I can leave but I'll make you explain it to him."

Eve shook her head. "Oh no, he's your handful." Caiden wasn't about to protest that. She opened the gate for him and motioned him to the house. "He's just out back setting up. Coffee?"

"My savior," Caiden replied, to which she simply tutted. "I'm serious! I'm usually rushing out the door and even today, I didn't manage to get more than one cup in." He followed her inside, instantly charmed by how every other corner was stuffed full of plants and art and shiny little things. "Okay, I love everything in here. It's a magpie's dream."

Eve rolled her eyes — and Caiden recognized it instantly from his time with Holland — but held out a full cup of nearly black coffee. He knew it was good stuff; she'd offered them coffee their first day on the job and every day afterwards. Caiden inhaled gratefully. "Well, I'm glad you appreciate it. Sometimes I wonder if it's too cluttered, but when I try to part with anything, I can't do it."

Caiden trailed his fingers through the dangling tendrils of spider plant near his left shoulder and swallowed several mouthfuls before replying. "Well, I'm just a stranger but honestly, I could spend hours here looking at everything. You said you were in academics, right? Is all this from your research days?"

When Eve didn't reply, Caiden glanced over. She was standing by the kitchen counter, her petite frame outlined in soft autumn morning sunshine, and she was smiling in that way older women had who weren't maybe the most forthcoming. It was a smile that said a lot, and again, he was reminded of Holland. There was zero physical resemblance, but clearly he'd been raised by this woman. It was sweet and made him think about Dee, his grandmother who had passed well over a decade ago.

Before either of them could speak again, the door to his left opened, hinges squealing the whole way, and there was Holland. Caiden was reintroduced to those long, lean lines of his physique all over again because the man was wearing absurdly tight skinny jeans, scuffed motherfucker boots in dark brown, and a flannel shirt with the sleeves rolled up to his elbows.

Holland gave them both a once-over, dark eyes lingering on Caiden long enough to make his ego swell. "I see you've already been introduced," Holland said. "She must like you, Caiden. She doesn't give out that coffee to everyone."

Caiden held back a laugh, but barely. Eve wasn't fairing much better. "Then she must like my crew, because your lovely Gamma has been offering it to us every day on the job."

And he waited for the pieces to click into place.

Holland didn't laugh or make some kind of outward sign of surprise. He nodded, tongue swiping over his lips, and said, "Of course she hired the place you work for."

"They're the best in town," Eve replied while pressing a thermos into Holland's hands. "So, you have the morning, and then Caiden's crew is coming out this afternoon to wrap up."

"And that's our cue to get to work," Holland said with a smile to Caiden. "Come on, let's get you set up."

Caiden made to follow Holland out the door, but Eve said, "I never answered your question. And yes, they are. The things all around you are largely from places I've traveled. Little bits of experiences I've been lucky enough to have." She held out a small oval stone, its iridescence mesmerizing. "A man in a pub in Wales gave this to me. He told me it would help balance my energies. I was newly separated and moping about while working on some research on Welsh mythology, so I took myself down to the pub for a drink."

Gingerly, Caiden took the stone. The play of colors across its smooth surface was impossible to ignore; light refracting in a way that felt almost alien. "Take it," she said with a smile. "Goodness knows I have plenty of things lying about. And it suits you."

"Suits me?"

"I think so."

Caiden rubbed his thumb over the stone and nodded. He'd digest the gesture later, when he was alone and staring at the ceiling while waiting for his body to relax enough to sleep. He'd learned some meditation techniques ages ago, as part of intensive therapy for his anxiety, and learning to relax his body before his mind had been a game changer. And having a new object to focus on might be good for the times when his old demons reared their ugly heads. "I guess a little energy balancing never hurt anyone. Thank you, Eve."

She looked pleased as he tucked the stone into his pocket, but thankfully didn't linger on the sentiment. "Come in any time for more coffee."

When Caiden finally stepped outside, the cool wind took him by surprise. Holland seemed unbothered. "Apologies ahead of time if you're still willing to have water dumped on you in this," he said as he motioned to the rectangular kiddie pool anchored down by rocks in the corners. "We'll do it last, so you can change and warm up."

"I'm down," Caiden said. "Where do you want to start?"

Holland walked him through some basic shots. More posing with a shovel, hands gripped suggestively on the old wood handle; him stretching with his hands behind his head, so his biceps flexed and his shirt rode up. Holland made it fun, encouraged Caiden to go with the flow and do what felt natural.

So, of course, he had to hone in on that. "You really have a way with people," Caiden mused as he put the flat blade of one hand to his forehead, as if he were blocking the sun.

"Turn toward me a little? Okay, a little more. Perfect." The camera shutter clicked three, four, seven times before Holland replied. "And thanks. I'm one of those extroverted introverts. I find people fascinating, but exhausting."

Caiden nodded. "I get that. I think some of that comes with age, too. At least for me."

Holland stepped back to check his laptop, which was perched on top of the case for all his equipment. "Were you a party animal back in the day?"

The teasing, lingering note, almost sultry — like salt on the rim of a margarita glass — had Caiden shifting a little. This guy was half art genius, half accidentally (maybe a little bit on purpose) a flirt. And fuck, it was *fun*. When was the last time he'd had fun like this?

Mind made up, Caiden replied as smoothly as possible. "Maybe a bit. Nothing too wild, but I had my fair share of mischief."

"Hmmm. I'm curious."

Caiden watched Holland walk over to his camera, make a small adjustment, then approach, his arms crossed easily over his chest. His stomach was doing that weird fluttery mating dance again, but there was a sizzle to it now. A gentle wave of energy up his spine. It was a *good* feeling and Caiden wanted to keep it going.

"Curious about what?" he asked, a flirty smile on his face. "My bad boy days?"

"Well, yes, but honestly? Right now?" Holland leaned down, bringing all that delicious height and the scent of coffee with him, and softly said, "I'm curious if you want to be Mr. June or Mr. July for the calendar. Because I think you're perfect for both."

Caiden's mind raced, but what fell out of his mouth was, "What's the difference?"

Holland's smile transformed into an all-knowing smirk that *did things* to Caiden. He wanted to know what that flannel would feel like under his hands and if Holland's knees were as sharp as they looked. Would they still be sharp if he ran his tongue over them on the way up to the softer, sweeter skin inside of his thighs —

"I was hoping Mr. July would be shirtless. Give the calendar buyers a little thrill right in the middle."

Fuck.

Slapped right out of his daydream, Caiden stared at Holland.

"Holy shit, you are *flirty*," he said, half-laughing and absolutely grinning up to his ears. "I thought last session was suggestive but wow, you really go for it."

Holland didn't hesitate. "And you showed up today. I took that as a good sign." But the flirty little look dropped from his face as he said, "But seriously, I don't want to make you uncomfortable. Please tell me to stop or dial it back or shut the hell up if I'm —"

Caiden stepped forward until he was inches from Holland. The proximity forced him to look up, otherwise he'd be staring at the man's collarbone, but the little thrill he got from it wasn't hidden in his voice. "I'm not the type of guy to stay quiet if something's bothering me," he said. He wanted to touch but didn't dare. Not now, when the moment was spun-glass fragile and prettier than the bit of stone at the bottom of his pocket. "But I'm also pretty aware of where we are and what we're supposed to be doing. So, I'll make you a deal. Let's do this thing today, and then I'll text you tonight. We can make some plans from there."

Holland hadn't so much as *touched him*, but Caiden could feel the energy between them. It felt a lot like the brush of fingers across his jaw or down his neck. "Sounds good," Holland said. He swallowed hard and Caiden took that as a positive.

Caiden stepped back, breaking the moment, and took a deep breath. Then, leaning on his shovel, fingers of one hand curled around the hem of his shirt, he said, "Tell me where you want me."

Chapter 7

Waiting sucked, so Holland was again staring at his photo board and his phone was across the room on his bedside table. If it was in his hand or his pocket, he'd be flicking it on every few seconds or staring at the half-composed text waiting for him to finish.

Waiting *sucked*, but he was holding Caiden to his promise of a text that night. To set up...a date? They hadn't really nailed that down, and Holland was desperate to find out if that was the plan.

Caiden. God. That man was...*something*. Something *different* and *fun* and *lively*. So opposite from him. Holland always framed himself as someone who loved working with people but also loved being alone, and since his skill set meant he needed people to make money, it all worked out. He would take photos, talk to customers, then go home and spend hours in the quiet dark, editing and piecing together other people's special moments and memories.

And admittedly, on the darker days when sleep had eluded him for long stretches of time, he felt a little bitter about the whole thing. Jaded, maybe, too. When was the last time something photograph-worthy happened in his life? Was he in a rut, stagnating in a job that brought others so much joy? He knew he couldn't live without his version of art and creation, but seeing so many other people grinning and hugging and *loving* each other left him a tad melancholy.

Holland sighed and stepped back from the board. This wasn't doing his mental state any good. Waiting and musing and feeling down was not healthy. He glanced out the window facing the quiet street, where the dark was pockmarked by circles of yellow sodium lights from the streetlamps, and made a decision.

Five minutes later, he was out the door, keys and phone in his coat pocket and a note left by the tea kettle in case Gamma awoke for her own insomnia-induced cup of oolong. They might not be blood, but they were certainly a lot alike, and he knew Gamma was prone to late night musings of her own. Leaving the note was his way of reassuring her.

The first real taste of winter hit him as he walked; the wind had a bitter edge and it scraped across his unprotected face. It also distracted his busy brain long enough to let go of that feeling of emptiness to wonder if he should just text Caiden. It was only ten p.m., early for him, but Caiden probably had to get up with the sun to hit job sites early.

After a couple of blocks, Holland stopped under a streetlight and pulled out his phone. He really shouldn't have worried so much, and clearly he'd been in his head, because there was a text from fifteen minutes ago. He felt like an ass.

> **CAIDEN:** So, here's the deal. I was too chicken to ask you out today, thought it might not be appropriate given we were doing a thing.

> **CAIDEN:** And maybe a text this late is not smart. But I'm hoping you see this.

> **CAIDEN:** Would love to meet up. For a date. I've got an idea on that, too, so you don't

have to do any work.

CAIDEN: How do you feel about mini golf? Cause I need to defeat that stupid pirate ship at the end of Mini Golf A Go-Go. At this point it's a blood vendetta. But we can also do something more normal, like food and the boardwalk.

Holland burst out laughing. Caiden really was fun, and the back-to-back texts were hopefully a sign of nerves on his end, too.

HOLLAND: I'm a jerk, didn't see this when it came through. Was too busy being in my head. So that's a thing I do, just up front. But I'd love to meet up and help you wage war on the pirate ship. Food is also a good idea, but it doesn't need to be fancy. I just got out of wedding season and ate so much shitty catered food that was probably crazy expensive.

HOLLAND: Also up front…I'm terrible at mini golf. Anything that requires hand-eye coordination outside a camera, actually.

The ellipses of death blinked and blinked while Holland gripped his phone.

CAIDEN: YESSSS I've recruited you into my war. We'll make it official on…Saturday? Or Sunday? Quick, I know, but I'm not a patient person. That's my up front for you. And if you're down for burritos, I know a place.

Holland couldn't help but grin. Caiden's whole vibe was sort of ageless, in that way that he was an adult but still knew how to have fun. Maybe Caiden could teach him a thing or two about relaxing and letting his guard down. He'd already done so many things with and around him that felt that way. He'd *flirted, blatantly,* on the job with this man, and made a few very suggestive jokes. He hadn't truly thought about it, just acted on impulse. And yeah, okay, a bit of lust, too.

He had a thing for shorter guys and Caiden had the added bonus of piercings. And he was fun and confident but not cocky.

HOLLAND: Count me in. But let me pick you up. Can't have you doing all the work.

CAIDEN: I'm into it. I also like that I'm the wordy one and you cut right to the chase. Can't help it, I'm a chatty guy, but I know when to turn it off. I think. I hope so.

CAIDEN: So, you're awake. So am I. What are you doing right now?

Good point. What *was* he doing right now? He'd set out to pull his head out of his ass and not mope around, and thankfully Caiden had all his attention at the moment. Holland bit his lip, let the wind buffet him about, then began to walk again. It took him a few moments to compose a reply that didn't sound asinine.

HOLLAND: I was walking around the neighborhood. Old habit when I can't get my brain to shut off. But now I'm talking to you.

CAIDEN: Cool, cool. Want to play twenty questions? Get to know each other a little better? I figure that might be the ticket, since you've already seen me shirtless and soaking wet.

Oh, those ellipses were working overtime as Caiden wrote back. Doubt crept into Holland's mind (was he being too flirty again, did he press the wrong button, and all that bullshit), but Caiden's reply was a needle to his balloon of anxiety.

Holland burst out laughing. This guy was matching him step for step and damn if it wasn't a blast.

Where was his sense of adventure? When had that gotten buried?

For the first time in a while, Holland chose not to overthink it. Act. Do. Be. Live.

It took a few tries to get the angle right, with how little light there was, but Holland snapped the picture and sent it. He hadn't grabbed a scarf on his way out, so it only took sliding the zipper down on his coat to expose his throat. The image was simple: his hand gently resting on his neck to show off his favorite feature: his sharp jawline. It was a physical trait he'd inherited from his mom, and he'd had many a date compliment it. Might as well use it to his advantage.

Caiden immediately reacted, sending exclamation marks and open-mouthed emojis back, but he followed it up with actual words.

you're hot and I'm very down with guys at least a head taller than me but I can tell you're a photographer. You should frame this picture and submit it somewhere. Holy shit, Holland.

Holland let out a breath and let his head fall back against the streetlight post. It was *nice* to be appreciated. And he wanted more of it. There was Caiden again, a compliment framed by appreciation for his artistic talents.

HOLLAND: You sure know how to make a guy blush. Pick you up on Saturday? Say 7 p.m.?

CAIDEN: Absolutely. But burritos and mini-golf are on me. Besides being a gentleman, I gotta pay you back for the photo somehow. I mean…wow.

CAIDEN: Is it too soon to tell you how hot you are?

Oh, there was that delicious tension again. It had bubbled up between them so quickly and left on a simmer, but now Holland wanted more. And clearly Caiden did, too. He felt like a giddy teenager on his first date. Except now, instead of hoping for an awkward kiss at the front door, he could just…invite someone back to his place or go to theirs. They could do whatever they wanted. Holland missed that feeling, that connection, and yes, the thrill of discovering someone's body and learning their shape, their taste.

Maybe Caiden could help him find it again.

HOLLAND: No, because I'm attracted to you, too.

CAIDEN: Whew, that's good. So, this won't be a pity date. Thank god.

HOLLAND: Not at all. And I think this would have happened even if I hadn't seen you with your shirt off.

Holland was now walking toward his place, could see the kitchen light in the back window, when his phone rang, Caiden's name on the screen.

"So here's the thing," Caiden said, all but purring into the line and setting Holland's nerves on fire, "this flirting is really fun. And I think you're fun. And I know Saturday is tomorrow so we're literally in the twenty-four-hour window. Less, actually. But...damn, Holland, you are something else. Where the hell did you come from?"

Caiden's words tumbled over themselves, eager to be next in line, and Holland was instantly charmed all over again. This guy clearly had a brain that went a mile a minute and he understood that. He was definitely more relaxed than Holland, but Holland knew anxiety when he heard it.

"I could say the same about you," Holland replied as he dug his keys out of his pocket. "I didn't expect a ripped landscaper to volunteer his time for a charity calendar. Especially not one who I clicked with immediately."

Caiden's little laugh rumbled down the line and it hit Holland right in the stomach. "Lucky us, I guess. I won't keep you. I know it's late." A pause, leaving Holland a moment to get inside and toe off his boots. "But I uh...I wanted to say thanks. You were cool from the beginning, even with as awkward as I was. And since I've already told you you're hot, I figured I'd call and say it again so you can hear it right from me."

Holland took the stairs to his room two at a time, eager and wide awake, his body buzzing with energy. "Keep complimenting me and I might have to do something about it."

"That a promise?"

Holland carefully, quietly, shut the door to his room, then flopped onto his bed. The phone was pressed tightly to his ear, to the point where he could feel his heartbeat through the cartilage, but he didn't dare put it on speakerphone and wake Gamma up. Plus, he wanted Caiden to really hear this.

"Maybe. Maybe I've got a thing for shorter guys with nipple piercings who might be amenable to being pressed against a wall and kissed hard and long. How's that sound?"

The sharp intake of breath on the other end was all the answer Holland needed, but Caiden, ever chatty, managed to say, "I think you better keep that promise."

"Then I will. Remember that tomorrow."

"I will if you will.

Caiden lived about fifteen minutes away, so Holland made sure he left right on time. His tendency to arrive early to *everything* could lead to some awkward situations, and he wasn't about to show up on a date and idle in the parking lot of Caiden's apartment complex. He wasn't *that* weird. He also had to fight the urge to fuss with his hair or twist the ring around his index finger. Both were nervous habits and he refused to be nervous. But of course, he was bouncing his leg to the beat of the 90s alt station, so the energy was going *somewhere*.

Holland spotted Caiden exiting the building, peer around the parking lot, and alight on his bright blue pickup. A truck sitting above mostly sedans and minivans was pretty obvious, and as soon as Caiden saw it, he grinned and bounded over.

"Guessing this thing is good for hauling your equipment around," Caiden said as he opened the passenger door and hopped in. "And also, hi. You look incredible."

Holland reached out to him without thinking, then pulled back. "So do you." And Caiden really did, in a lime green puffer jacket, black cords, and what looked like a dark green shirt peeking through where the zipper wasn't done up. He looked colorful and fun and *dangerous* at the same time, if Holland was being a little dramatic about it. He hadn't fussed too much about his own clothing (or else he risked spending *all day* trying on everything), but layers were a necessity for the weather and mini golf.

"Well, it's not exactly caftan weather, so I did my best," Caiden replied as Holland put the truck in gear. When Holland burst out laughing, Caiden simply grinned and said, "Now you're picturing it, so let's get it right. My favorite caftan is Malibu blue with these peachy coral flowers on it, it's gay as hell, and I only wear it at home when it's like ninety degrees outside."

The question was right on the tip of his tongue and Holland almost couldn't believe he was going to say it. "Is there anything under the caftan?"

"Hell no. What would be the point when the weather's that hot?"

They both giggled like little kids and Holland took that chance to give Caiden another quick once-over. "I've never experienced the pleasure but it sounds nice."

Caiden wiggled in his seat and, with a nod from Holland, adjusted the two vents on his side. He put his hands up against them with a sigh. "It's fabulous. But that's the kind of thing I do for myself, you know? When you work with people all day, you have to adhere to certain standards, but at home, everything's fair game. A friend of mine who used to room with me left her caftan behind when moving and I tried it on. With her permission, of course. And that was it."

Holland stopped for a red light and finally got to look over properly at Caiden again. "I can see it. You floating around your place and just feeling good about yourself. It sounds nice."

Caiden nodded. "It is. I turned forty six months ago and let me tell you, my give a fucks — what's left of them — flew out the window."

He had to laugh at that. "Is that what happens at milestone birthdays? What's that saying...the fields in which our fucks are grown get plowed over? Something like that."

"Sounds about right. Though I prefer salting the ground so nothing can ever grow there again. I'd rather uh...plant new fields, if we're continuing the metaphor."

Holland almost missed the light turning green, he was so wrapped up in their conversation and stepped on the gas a little too quickly. They jolted forward to the sound of an irritated honk behind them. "Whoops. Apparently, I'm a little nervous."

"So am I."

The rest of the drive to mini golf was peppered with steady conversation, and eventually Holland relaxed into its rhythm. Caiden made it easy, as he gave and took in equal amounts and seemed genuinely curious about Holland. By the time they got to the mini-golf course and Holland parked alongside the old wooden fence separating the parking lot from a bit of wooded area, he finally felt settled.

Of course, that's when Caiden surprised him.

Holland made to hop out of the truck, but Caiden stopped by with a simple, "Hey, got a question for you."

Holland pulled the door shut and turned in his seat so they were face to face. "Yeah, sure."

Caiden cocked his head, a curious light in his eyes. "When you picked me up, you reached out to me, but pulled back after a second. I just wanted to let you know that it's okay. To touch me. If I don't want something, I'll say it."

And then he leaned in and Holland felt that low-slung tightening in his gut. A promise of *more*. Of something exciting and new, and it was bundled up in a bright green puffer coat and smiling at him. "Especially since I didn't forget what you said last night. And I'm big on consent. Granted, I haven't had a lot of practice lately, but I try to respect people's space. But I'm also a big touchy-feely guy, so if you want to link arms or even hold hands, I'm down. And if you want to press me into some wall later tonight, maybe outside a dive bar that has a killer pool table, or up against my door, I'm down for that, too."

Caiden's big brown eyes were gorgeous in any light, but Holland was getting the up close and personal treatment right now; he could see the little ring of hazel around Caiden's pupils and the glint of the blue studs in his ears. And he was warm and real and so close, and Holland didn't want to stop. Not here. Not now.

Not when Caiden was looking at him like that. Now when he'd just said all *that* and clearly meant every word.

Holland reached up, no hesitation this time, and curled his fingers and palm around Caiden's jaw. "How about this?" Holland asked softly. "Is this okay?"

"Got me in the palm of your hand," Caiden said. "And yeah, it's more than okay. So...now what?"

That bubbly excitement had Holland pushing forward and pressing his lips to Caiden's. Nothing scandalous, just a warm mouth against his own and a warm hand cupped around the one he had on Caiden's jaw. But it felt *good*.

Holland had to let him go after a few seconds. The temptation to keep going was strong. But he'd burned himself and pushed away others by moving too fast, and honestly…. why rush it? Why not *savor* it?

"Careful," Caiden said as soon as Holland pulled away. "Much more of that and I'm going to be finding out how far back those seats recline."

"That would suck for both of us, since they don't," Holland replied.

Caiden burst out laughing. "Ugh, okay, yes that would massively suck. Good call. And I wouldn't get my last shot this year at revenge on that pirate ship. The mini golf closes down for the season in a few days."

"Well, we can't have that."

They got out of his truck and headed toward the entrance for the course, deciding to split a basket of balls. When Holland asked why they didn't need another basket, Caiden said, "I'm trying to work the power of positive thinking on this damn place. Every time I'm here, everyone gets their own basket. I've never just used half a basket. I've tried everything else to improve my game, so now I'm relying on bullshit."

Holland chuckled and handed Caiden their clubs. "I used to be a pretty good bullshitter, so maybe it will work."

"My lucky charm," Caiden said as he pressed a hand to his chest.

They got to the first hole, a simple practice putt lined by tall hedges, so you (hopefully) didn't lose a ball. Caiden took the basket of golf balls and watched while Holland lined up his shot.

"So, you said you've tried everything to get past the pirate ship," Holland said as he tapped his club against the ball, waiting until it smoothly dropped into the hole before continuing. "And if I'm the lucky charm...what happens to that free one-year membership I saw advertised as the prize for doing that?"

Caiden's grin was wide and playful. "Depends on who sinks it."

"So I don't get lucky charm credit if you do?"

Caiden closed the space between them, immediately curling his hand into Holland's collar. "I'll give you whatever you want, handsome. But that membership is mine."

Holland leaned down, unable to keep from grinning. "You drive a hard bargain," he said before brushing his lips against Caiden's. Just a tease. Just enough to make them both *want* a little more fiercely. He hoped by the end of the night that *want* would turn into something more.

Chapter 8

CAIDEN

Caiden watched as Holland walked around the ninth hole putting green. The mini-golf place only had twelve holes, and the ninth was the next hardest outside that damn pirate ship. But somehow, despite being truly *terrible* at mini golf, his date had gotten to the ninth hole in one shot.

One.

"I still can't believe you did that," Caiden muttered as Holland squared up to his ball. The reason everyone hated this hole was the multi-tiered design. It was like shooting pool on a 5-D table right out of some sci-fi show. By a stroke of wild luck, Holland's ball had progressed through the clear tunnel up to the triangular, tiered structure, then clanked its way back down through the succession of holes to come back out the other side, resting just a few feet from the hole.

Holland threw him a grin. One that had Caiden leaning a little harder on the garden wall separating them from the rest of the course. "You did say I might be your lucky charm."

"Oh, I'm confident of it now. Absolutely."

Caiden didn't miss the extra wiggle Holland put in his hips as he pulled the club back. The ball sank into the hole, landing with a satisfying *click* into the cup. Holland turned back to him, smug triumph on his face. "And now?"

In another version of their timeline, Caiden confidently strode up to Holland, took the club from his hand, and let it drop to the ground while he pressed his mouth to the sharp cut of Holland's jaw. His earlier lingering touch there had made Holland shiver and Caiden wanted to feel it again. "Now I'm just wanting to go beat that damn pirate ship so I can properly reward my lucky charm."

Holland's soft little groan was choked by his laugh. "Promises, promises."

The tenth and eleventh holes were pretty straightforward, and he'd long conquered them, so Caiden was content to watch Holland step up to the plate, so to speak. He'd always been fairly good at reading people, and Holland was clearly the studious type. Someone who didn't rush into decisions. But it was hard to miss the lingering glances Holland was sending his way and Caiden really hoped this early compatibility — and attraction — between them wouldn't fatigue as the night wore on.

"And now the main event," Caiden said as they walked down the set of stairs to the very large animatronic pirate ship set in a pond where waterspouts went off every two minutes. "It's one of the last mini golf challenges designed by this company, Lionstone Golf, before it went out of business. You have to get your ball up the gangplank, across the ship, and miss all the little characters that are triggered when your ball rolls by. Oh, and also hope that you don't hit it too hard and land in the pond, or get your ball taken out by a waterspout."

There was another pair ahead of them, a woman with a long braid down her back and another, younger girl. The older person was lining up a shot, so Caiden motioned for Holland to scoot to the side, so they didn't interrupt.

As soon as the woman hit her ball, Caiden knew immediately that it was a goner. Ideally, you could clear the pirate ship in three or four putts, but her first hit didn't have enough speed to move it past the little pirates and their cutlasses.

"Doesn't look good," Holland whispered in his ear. "You're grimacing."

"Am I that obvious?"

"Terribly." Holland slid his arm over Caiden's shoulder and pulled him closer. Caiden tried to not snuggle in too much, since Holland was a tall wall of warmth and the sun was just starting to set, making the breeze even colder.

The woman's ball landed in the pond and she slumped forward, but slowly moved away from the tee so they could step up.

After they had disappeared around the corner, Holland whistled. "This thing is devious. No wonder you want to try to beat it."

There was a much longer story there, but nothing Caiden felt like rehashing right now. Not on a first date, when they were keeping it light and fun. Maybe he'd tell Holland in the future, if this thing between them kept going. He tried to be a realist; dating at any age was difficult and Caiden wasn't interested in doing casual dates all the time. It got boring and expensive and felt so superficial.

Was it so bad to want connection with someone else? More than just the sex (okay, sex was great, but it wasn't the focus). More than the nights out. He wanted the little domestic dream, him and someone else and maybe a pet and a kitchen that always smelled like something good was waiting in the oven.

When he didn't immediately answer, Holland nudged him. "You okay?"

"Yeah, I'm good. Just trying to time the waterspouts." Caiden pointed to them. "There's about two seconds after the last one stops that you have to get your ball going the exact right speed to clear all the obstacles. And that's if those damn pirates don't knock it into the water."

"Well, I believe in you." And from the way Holland was smiling at him, Caiden figured he was telling the truth.

"And I appreciate it. Well, no time like the present."

Caiden placed his ball on the tee and waited for the last waterspout.

One...two...

The ball followed course, going up the gangplank, narrowly avoiding the little moving pirate feet and cutlasses, and just passed over the first waterspout before coming to rest just inside the ship.

Caiden tried not to look too excited. "First part complete! Whew. I thought that one pirate had it out for me."

He led Holland up the human-sized gangplank and into the hollow ship, where the more tightly constrained space made the next hit even more difficult. He showed Holland all the various pitfalls and traps, then put his ball down and stepped back. "This is where I get stuck about eighty percent of the time. So, fingers crossed."

Holland winked at him. "You've got this."

Was it silly to be nervous about a damn mini golf course? Of course it was. And yet some part of him reveled in it, because this place, and this particular mini golf hole, was special. He really wanted to beat it, just one time.

Caiden focused on shutting out all the sounds — the rushing water, the click-clack of the gears moving the pirates along their tracks, the furious beating of his own heart — and waited for the exact moment.

When the ball smoothly rolled across the ship's interior and managed to make it to the other side, where a tunnel would take it down to the final part of the challenge, Caiden was *thrilled*. "Oh, hell yes, I can't believe that worked!"

Holland was looking around, confusion written across his face. "Wait, where did it go?"

"Come on, I'll show you."

He walked them back outside, to where the final part of the challenge waited. It was a deceptively simple end to the twelfth hole; a putting green lined with wood slats set at various diagonal angles.

"It's like a minotaur maze or something," Holland mused as they stared over the putting green. "This is almost cruel. You go through all that to get to this?"

"Yep. And by this point you're so fried, one little slip-up means you don't get to the other side because you over or under-shot your putt." He pointed out all the other holes at the ends of the wood slats. "I've failed somewhere on all of these so many times, but I've been practicing. I even have a little putting green in my spare bedroom."

After he put his ball down, Holland snagged him by the arm and leaned in. "For luck."

Caiden accepted the kiss eagerly, anxious to pour some of his energy into anything other than the final challenge. The gentle press of Holland's lips took the edge off, and he was hesitant to pull away.

"Here goes nothing," Caiden said as he pulled his club back.

The ball took off with speed (another trick you had to get right to keep from getting the ball lodged in between the wood slats or stuck in a corner) and zipped through the first two diagonal tracks, but when it reached the third, it bounced off the wood and arched over the fourth. Caiden groaned and made to look away, but Holland pointed and said, "Holy shit, Caiden."

The ball hit the green in the fifth diagonal track, pinged off the sixth, and shot right through the seventh, and final. Caiden stood there, gaping like a fish, struck by the weird luck of missing a whole set of slats and still making it so close to the hole…because his ball rolled to a stop two inches from it.

"No way," Caiden breathed, still staring. "No way that worked."

"Sure looks like it did," Holland replied. "Does it count if you make the hole in four, instead of three, hits?"

"Yeah. You just have to make it there."

"Come on!" Holland all but dragged him over to his ball, grinning the whole way. "Finish the course! That was incredible, Caiden, holy shit. And you'll get your year membership."

They walked together to the last hole and stared down at his bright blue putt-putt ball. One little push and he'd have done something that had taken years. A wave of melancholy hit him all at once. Huh. He really thought he'd feel happier about this.

"I'm getting the feeling it's not just about winning," Holland said softly as they stared.

"It's not," Caiden managed to say. "A story for another time. Gotta leave some mystery for you to try to unravel on future dates, right?"

Holland took him by the chin and tipped his face up. "I'm game if you are."

All it took was one little tap of the ball into the cup with barely a twitch of his club.

There were no flashing lights or music to notify everyone around of his accomplishment. He didn't want or need that. There were security cameras all over the place and he knew the staff would review the footage to see him sink that final putt. Before they headed to the front desk to claim the membership, Caiden held out his ball to Holland and asked, "Care to give the pirate ship a try? You only putted at eleven holes."

"No need. I just saw you do something completely wild. I am not going to come even close to stacking up to that. But I also do not want to steal your thunder." As they reached the front counter, Holland pointed at the screens overhead. A handful of employees had gathered to watch a loop of Caiden's victory putt, and one of them raised a fist in the air and said, "Nice job, man!".

"I mean, it's a personal victory but is it egotistical of me to be sort of glad someone else saw it in real time?" Caiden asked. "I feel a little silly about the whole thing, always have, but…"

Holland steered him a few feet away and took him gently by the shoulders. "Question for you, and I'm really being serious right now."

The shift in tone made Caiden worried. "Okay."

"Did you have fun sinking that putt?"

"Yeah, of course."

Holland shook his head. Some of his dark blonde hair had slowly escaped his ponytail as the wind had whipped around them all night and Caiden wanted to reach up, smooth it back into place. "So, I'm hoping you hear me when I say that's all that matters. You had fun, and you did something really cool. I bet anything they're going to watch that on repeat until this place shuts down for the season. Don't weigh your accomplishments based on anything else other than how you feel about it. Mini golf, cutting a hedgerow just right, taking the perfect picture. Lean into it, Caiden."

Then Holland ran his fingers across the shaved part behind Caiden's ear and whispered, "You timed it *just right* and had to factor in every moving part of that course. If it helps, I found that pretty hot."

Maybe he would tell Holland the whole story behind the pirate ship sooner rather than later. Holland might just understand and wouldn't that be something.

Caiden snagged the year pass from an employee, signed his name to a very short list of people who had ever made it all the way through that damn twelfth hole, and said, "Want to grab a drink? I'm parched."

Holland jangled his truck keys in reply. "Got some place in mind?"

"Oh, I absolutely have the right spot."

The right spot was the diviest dive bar on that side of town, a lone brick building sandwiched in by a dry cleaner and a veterinary office.

"It was actually the first bar built in town, the third building to be constructed. After the sheriff's office and a bank," Caiden said as they took their beers over to the pool table that wasn't in use. "I hung out here a lot in college, got to know the owner, Nat. Her family has owned the place for decades."

He traded his bottle for a cue and handed another one to Holland, getting to admire those artist's hands in low amber light. It hadn't taken him long to notice the big signet ring on his right index finger. It was a pretty thing of silver and a dark blue stone cabochon, and he was curious. Maybe it was the magpie in him, always finding the shiniest thing to admire. Plus, there wasn't any other jewelry (that he could see right now) on the man, while Caiden routinely changed the jewelry in his piercings just because he liked the variety. And being shiny.

Holland wanted to break, so he racked the balls and stood back to watch Holland line up his shot. "I like that your brain seems to be full of trivia. Especially about the city," Holland said after the balls bumped to a stop. "I came back about five years ago. Gamma was going to sell the house if she didn't have some help, so I took over the maintenance stuff for the house after I moved in."

"Except for the gardens," Caiden said. "You know, I've met your Gamma three times, and I keep getting more impressed. Hell of a lady."

"She has that effect on people," Holland said, his smile warm and open. It was completely beyond adorable that he clearly loved Eve, and the feeling was obviously mutual. He took a slow sip of his stout, giving him time to admire Holland in the bar's shitty lighting. He looked somehow right at home and slightly out of place, an artist bundled up in preppy layers holding a bottle of local craft brew in one hand and pool cue in the other.

Caiden liked to people-watch, which was easy to do when you spent most of your working hours outside at nice houses in nice neighborhoods. Places that had neatly paved roads that joggers used and sidewalks for strollers and bikes and walkers. He'd see someone briskly walking and wonder if they were in a hurry or simply a fast walker, or catch glimpses of the people who lived in the house across the street and could guess at why their hatchback was so damn muddy. Did they camp? Mud run? Get stuck in a rainstorm and have to pull off to the side of the road to wait it out?

All that people watching had racked up to what he figured was a decent radar for most folks. And that's why he'd wanted to spend some time with Holland. The enigma of him. So professional, but drop a few flirty little glances his way, and Holland had responded in kind. He got the feeling that Holland wasn't the type of person to do something against his will. It would have been easy enough to let Caiden down gently and go about their merry, separate ways.

But instead, Holland had gone mini-golfing with him. Listened to his ranting about the pirate ship. Encouraged him to savor his victory. And now he was giving him a dark look that screamed *challenge*, and Caiden felt his blood heat.

"You a betting man, Holland?" Caiden asked as he slowly walked around the table. One dark blonde eyebrow went up and it was so ridiculous, and ridiculously *sexy*, and Caiden wasn't about to stop there. "Want to wager on who wins this one game of pool?"

Holland took a sip of his beer, then set it aside, motioning for Caiden to step up to the table. "What brought this on?"

That incredible look you gave me moments ago. The one that had me willing to go to my knees for you, and I never get on my knees unless they have a landscaping pad under them. "I'm riding high on my win against the pirate ship at mini-golf and looking to keep it going." He put both hands high up on his cue and leaned forward. "I can make it good for both of us no matter what. Promise."

There was that look again — molten hot and turning Caiden's insides to jelly. If his old knees could wobble, they'd be doing it right now. "Tempting," Holland drawled and for the first time, Caiden caught the slightest twinge of an accent. He'd need to hear more of it to be sure, because the bar had all kinds of background noise and the guys at the pool table beside them had begun to *really* drink and carry on.

Another little bit of mystery, another fun thing to discover about Holland. Caiden liked the chase as much as anyone, but what he really craved anymore was connection and romance. Maybe it was age, maybe it was because he was wiser now. But he just wanted to be *near* someone and get to know them, touch them, and have them be interested in him like that, too.

"Yeah?" Caiden shot him a grin. "Okay, first wagers on the table, then. If I win this game of pool in this slightly grungy, somehow weirdly damp bar, then I get to photograph you. Say a dozen photos, your choice of the *when* and *how* and all that. You'll get to pose for me."

Holland's expression morphed into curiosity. "Why that?"

Caiden shrugged. "Honestly? I've wanted to do it since we met, cause who takes pictures of the photographer? You're so steady behind the camera and you clearly love what you do. I got curious as to what that would look like if the roles were flipped."

After a long moment, Holland laughed, bent over so one hand was on the pool table's worn edge. "Okay, okay," he said after a few seconds, hand pressed to his cheek, where his pale skin had gone pink, "I was not expecting that. Though I should have figured you'd be all kinds of surprising, given this has been the most creative, memorable date from my end of things. But I accept your terms."

Excitement buzzed in his veins and had Caiden shifting from foot to foot. "Okay, cool, but what about you? What if you win?"

A little flicker of tongue, just enough to dampen Holland's lips, had Caiden sucking in a breath. "First of all, if this isn't all right by you, just say so. Boundaries are boundaries and I'm firm on that. But honestly..." That gaze raked up and down Caiden's body, growing hotter by the second. "I kind of had the same idea. Who gives the landscaper beauty in his life?" When Caiden opened his mouth to ask what the hell that meant, Holland said, "What I really want is to take you back to mine and massage what I know are probably very sore muscles. You spend all day making other people's lives brighter and better, and I can give you a bit of that tonight."

Then Holland swooped in, kissing-distance away and looking like he needed a good mussing. Caiden was more than happy to oblige, so he curled his fingers into Holland's collar once again and pulled him down. "So, if I win, I get a reward," he whispered, "and if I lose, I still get a reward."

"Maybe not as much as you expect, if you lose," Holland whispered back. "I have a thing for making people feel good."

"You get off on giving other people pleasure?"

Holland kissed his smirking mouth and Caiden melted into it. It was soft and sweet but far too short of a kiss. But a good one all the same. "Maybe," he teased, brushing his thumb over Caiden's chin. "Care to up the challenge a little?"

"Ooo, risky," Caiden teased back. "But let's say I'm curious."

"We hit until we miss rules, instead of that standard crap. So, every time your cue touches a ball, you can ask me a question. About anything. I'm a pretty open book. And vice versa, but only with what you're comfortable sharing." Holland was now dragging his thumb over the corner of Caiden's mouth and the temptation to pull it between his lips was hitting *hard*.

"Honestly? Sounds like fun. And same. I'm not one of those guys who claims to be an open book but is really finicky about what that means. Ask and I'll do my best to answer, even if it's to say 'I don't know'."

"And it incentivizes both of us to make our shots count," Holland said.

"I do like a smart man."

"Tease."

They managed to step away from each other, and Caiden went to stand on the other side of the table, where a corner stripe shot was nearly perfectly lined up. "You said you moved back to the city five years ago," he started as he eyed the shot from a few slightly different angles.

"I don't see your cue against the ball," Holland said with a grin.

"Patience, patience. I'm lining up my shot and my question." Satisfied with his spot, Caiden drew the cue back and took his shot. It was a good shot, but not great, and he only sank one of the two balls. "Good to know I'm rusty. Damn. So...where did you move from to good ol' Boston and/or the suburbs?"

Holland took a drink before answering. "Chicago. I worked for a marketing firm, mostly doing boring business shots. CEO portraits, team building days. Corporate shit, but it paid decently. I moved back when Gamma wanted to downsize but only because it was just her in the house. With me around, she could keep the house and have help."

Caiden's heart twisted at that. Holland clearly adored Eve, and how could you not admire someone who had given up part of their own life to be with someone they loved? "I just asked where you moved from. But thank you for telling me what you did."

Holland shrugged. "We're just playing, friendly and all. And besides, Gamma did so much for me, it was the least I could do to repay her. And I love Boston, always have. It's not like Chicago had better weather."

Caiden sputtered a laugh. "Fair. Ooof, yeah winter is brutal in both." He had another decent shot, but this one was tucked in close with a solid ball, and one little overshoot would send both spinning but not sinking. He wasn't a big competitive person or anything, but he was kind of curious about what questions Holland might ask. They *were* just getting to know each other, after all.

He knew the moment his cue touched the ball, it was a bad shot. The cue was old and worn and his hands were sweaty from nerves and excitement. The ball bounced off the stripe he was aiming for, then skipped across the table to knock a solid into the pocket.

"Fuck," he said, not really feeling it.

Holland stuck out his bottom lip and fake pouted. "Aw, that's so sad, now it's my turn. But you still have a question to ask."

Oh, he had several but the first one that Caiden blurted out was, "Vampires or werewolves? Who wins in a fight?"

Holland was angling up for his own shot but stilled and gave Caiden a wide-eyed stare. "Completely unexpected but I'll bite." Caiden just smiled at him and Holland shook his head with a laugh. "Honestly, hard choice for me, since I'm a fan of both. But probably vampires."

"Kinky. I like it."

"And werewolves aren't, with all that alpha and beta stuff?"

Caiden had to bite the inside of his cheek to keep from laughing. "Someone's been on the dark side of some fan fiction archives."

Holland wasn't fazed in the least. "You have no idea," he replied. "But if that's what you consider dark-sided for fan fic, I have a few stories to send you."

Oh, this was gold. One little question and Holland was opening up to him like a flower and it was *fun*. Caiden suddenly wanted to know everything about this man, and also maybe drag him into the bathroom or the back alley so he could suck his cock.

"I'll swap you bookmarks sometime. Maybe that's our second date. Takeout, beer, and bad fan fic."

As Holland lined up his shot, he paused to look up over his

extended arm, gaze locked on Caiden. "I'm in. But only if you read me your favorite one out loud."

Of fucking *course* the man was a pool master. His first shot knocked two solids into neighboring pockets. Caiden groaned and dramatically slapped his forehead. "Figures you're good at this. I thought you had shitty hand-eye coordination?"

The little eyebrow wiggle Holland gave him was far too sexy. It should have looked silly, but Caiden quickly realized nothing looked silly on him.

"I noticed the craft brew you picked," Holland said as he set up for his next shot. "Beer your drink of choice?"

It felt like a simple question. So naturally, Caiden leaned into it. "Only socially. I don't keep alcohol in the house. I come from a family of addicts, so when I was able to buy it legally, I swore I'd never bring it into wherever I lived. Socially it is fine, no more than two, never more than twice a week. But yeah, craft brews from local places are something a friend — Richie, the guy who's been helping at your Gamma's place, who also told me about this whole charity calendar thing? He got me drinking them. They're just different, which isn't always good, but at least it's not predictable."

Another look, this one as hot as ever but dancing with an edge of darkness that Caiden found he really liked, scraped over him. Holland took the shot and pocketed another solid, and that's when Caiden realized he was probably not getting another question in during the game.

And he was just fine with that.

"Let's do another easy one," Holland said as he straightened. "I'm just curious..."

The distance between them Holland covered in two strides of those long, long legs, and then he was towering over Caiden, pressing him into the wall. One hand flat on the worn brick, the other hovering over Caiden's chest. The scant air between them was immediately too warm and Caiden's stomach twisted with *need*. Holland didn't know it, but he was fuel on the fire of Caiden's long-banked desires; little hot-and-bothered dreams he tucked away for the right moment.

"Your place or mine?"

This man was going to kill him and Caiden was *ready*. "What about the bet?"

"Fuck the bet. You're getting a massage anyways, the bet just made it a little more thrilling in the moment." Holland was gentle when he ran his fingers across Caiden's jaw but it did nothing to dampen how badly he *wanted*. "And I'll pose for those photos. For you and only you."

"My place," Caiden said as he pushed up to put his mouth to Holland's pulse. "Let's give your Gamma a nice quiet night because the things I want to do to you are not quiet or polite in any way."

Chapter 9

"This is always the awkward part," Caiden said as Holland started his truck.

He sounded *nervous* and heaven help him, Holland found it endearing. He was nervous, too, but it came with an edge of confidence. He'd never had a lover complain about his prowess in bed, and given he used to have a thing for blunt talkers (back when he thought libertarianism was cool and edgy), and not one of them would have held back.

Caiden was a full head shorter than him. Compact, lean. But despite the attractiveness of his physical attributes, Caiden was exactly the kind of guy he loved having sex with. It was about *attitude*, and Caiden was a great combo of nerdy and perceptive; evidence of a sexy brain on top of a sexy body. Their conversation hadn't lulled once, and the whole night had felt easy. So why not keep the same through-line going? Why not keep it easy, even if it sounded like Caiden was nervous?

So before he pulled out of the bar's parking lot, truck idling, Holland turned to Caiden and put a hand on his arm. "I know you're sort of joking, because I'm pretty sure I can hear it in your voice...but I get it. I'm nervous, too. I spend so much time at work, and even when I'm not at work, I think about photography. Too busy to —"

"Have really great sex?" Caiden finished.

Holland laughed. "Oh, he's confident. But yes. Even to have sex. It's stupid, on one hand, cause I like sex. But I've never..." He trailed off, staring out the windshield. Shit, he'd really just started to say *all that*, and to someone he was on a first date with.

"I get it," Caiden said softly before putting a hand over Holland's. "Hey, I'm easy. If we get to my place and we just want to hang, I make a killer cup of tea. Or we make out on the couch like teenagers. Or we have sex. It's...I want it to be fun. Really."

Holland nearly breathed out a sigh of relief. Caiden had managed to allay a lot of his insecurities and fears in one go. And, realistically, there was always the chance that they were incompatible sexually. Or suddenly they didn't get along. Or maybe Caiden was really a bastard in disguise and this was how he lured guys back to his place.

But truthfully, Holland didn't believe any of that. So many years spent observing the smiles that turned sour the moment the camera lens was covered; the quiet joy in the eyes of people truly in love; the brightness in the face of a graduate who was so proud of their accomplishments. So many years watching people that it came naturally to him even now, when the slow fog of *need* began to roll in.

Still, he said, "It has been such an *easy* night that of course my stupid doubts are rising to the surface."

Caiden chuckled. "Join the club."

"Can I be the treasurer?"

Caiden's dark eyebrows went up at that. "I was gonna give you Vice President. Why the treasurer?"

Holland rubbed his thumb and index finger together. "The *mon-*

ey. The *power*."

Snickering, Caiden dug in his pocket and came out with a dime, a penny, and a handful of lint. "Here's our starting funds. What can you do with this, all mighty and powerful Treasurer of the Stupid Brains club?"

It really had been that simple to make the bit of tension and worry between them pop, and soon Holland had them down the road while Caiden told him a story about the time a guy called them in a panic because he tried to dig his own koi pond.

"People are wild," Holland said as he slid the truck into a spot at the edge of the lot attached to Caiden's building. The big parking lot light above them cast the cab in a golden glow. A bit of rain on the windshield drew Caiden's attention, and in that moment, Holland saw the perfect shot.

He held his phone up and when Caiden frowned at him, confused, Holland said, "The way the light was hitting your face as you looked out the windshield was perfect. Do you think you could –"

"Assume the position?" Holland's replying glare was toothless and from the way Caiden was grinning, he knew it, because he continued. "Oh, like you didn't see that coming a mile away."

"Actually, I didn't," Holland said, waiting until Caiden tipped his face up again before reaching out. "Here, like this," he said, softening his voice while he ran his thumb over Caiden's chin. "Perfect."

"Keep saying things like that, and I'll become a limpet and never leave." Caiden's big brown eyes were glued to his face, their little flickers of movement evidence that he was looking closely at Holland as Holland was at him. It should have made him feel weird or maybe self-conscious again, but instead, he felt warm. Happy. And yeah, fine, a little bit on the edge of aroused.

Holland finally let him go and took the picture. But when he turned the screen around to show Caiden the raw image, Caiden just shook his head. "How do you do it? I look...I don't know a word for it. It's me, but a little bit closer to *me* like I see myself. Cause every time I see a picture of myself someone else took, it's always a little..."

"Uncanny valley?" Holland offered. "Oh, I get it. So apparently, we as humans are primed to hate the sound of our own voice. I've always thought it's got to be something similar with most people and photos of themselves. I hear that sentiment a lot because a lot of people still aren't comfortable with their photo being taken, even when everyone has a tiny camera in their pocket."

He pinched his fingers on the screen to zoom in until Caiden's eyes were the center focus. The heat of Caiden's stare on him was starting to make the whole truck cabin feel a tad too warm and he fought against the urge to pull at his collar. Caiden's quiet intensity in the moments that truly counted was heady.

"So, I guess the point I'm trying to make here is that the people who photograph the best aren't the ones used to it. Your eyes were just too pretty in that light. I couldn't resist."

Caiden slowly let out a breath, unclipped his seat belt, and dug into his pockets to pull out a keyring. "You comin' up?"

Holland let his gaze drag up Caiden's body, lingering on his neck, then his lips. "If the offer's still open."

"You better believe it is. Turns out I have a thing for tall photographers who say my eyes are pretty."

The moment they met in front of his truck, Caiden grabbed his wrist and quick-walked them across the parking lot. Their steps were swallowed up by the rainy dark and while they weren't the only ones running from their cars to avoid the raindrops, it *felt* like they were alone. Holland's world was narrowed down to the warm clasp of fingers on his wrist and the way Caiden kept grinning back at him.

And when they were shoulder-to shoulder together in the building's small elevator, Holland felt the overwhelming need to press Caiden's back into that scuffed but clean mirror surface and kiss him. But people kept coming and going and Caiden waved to a few of them, apparently unaware of how badly Holland wanted him. Or maybe he was playing it cool, which was fair.

But Holland wanted to make sure, so the moment they were safely inside Caiden's apartment, he had that man's back up against the front door, his fingers curled into Caiden's coat collar. Caiden didn't get a word in edgewise. Couldn't, not with the way Holland was kissing him.

The clever fingers in his hair began to pull, sending hot little tingles across Holland's skin, and he leaned back, left panting for air between words. "So much for that drink."

Caiden let his head thunk back against his door. "Oh, we can have a drink, Holland. But *fuck*, give a man a minute." But his eyes were blazing. A challenge.

Holland did *not*. *Fuck, I hope I'm reading this right.* "I don't want the drink. I want you. But tell me to stop, and we stop."

Caiden yanked him in by the lapels and Holland sank into that kiss. He let his mind go blank for the first time in…he didn't even know how long but it didn't matter because Caiden's tongue was in his mouth and all that muscle was pressed up against him.

"Get this…off," Caiden muttered as he shoved at Holland's jacket. Pinned as he was, his attempt didn't do much, but Holland was quickly learning he liked the sight of Caiden all riled up. His cheeks had gone pink and his mouth red like a bruised cherry and the little piercings up and down his cartilage flickered in the little light that filtered in through the windows.

Holland stepped back to shrug out of his jacket and while Caiden was doing the same, he couldn't help but look around. The main room was all exposed brick and wood beams. Caiden had an L-shaped sofa up against a wall he guessed was the back of the kitchen, a modest TV and stereo set-up dominating the other wall. But every corner housed a bookshelf, each one brimming with volumes.

The nearest bookshelf was within arm's reach and Holland let his curiosity control his fingers as he danced them over the spines. "I'll give you the tour afterwards," Caiden said in his ear as he pressed up against Holland's back. And without the layers of clothing between them, Holland was finally able to feel the strength of Caiden's hands as Caiden felt him up.

"You feel good," Caiden murmured, his touch igniting trails of fire across Holland's chest. "And I gotta say, you are exactly my type."

"Smart and artsy?"

Caiden chuckled. "And a bit of a sass, too. But yeah, all of that. And how you look."

It slipped out before Holland really thought about it. "Like a green bean?"

"Self-deprecation is not allowed in this apartment." Caiden trailed a hand further down, until he reached the button on Holland's jeans. "I will hold out on you if you keep doing that, Holland." Caiden slipped around him so they could look at each other, and the intensity in his gaze left Holland's mouth dry. "You're gorgeous. I could say something slick like 'I don't sleep with people I'm not attracted to', which is true, but also..." He tugged on Holland's jeans. "You are *exactly* my type. Trust me."

Holland shifted in Caiden's hold, the whipcord strength of Caiden's arms like bands around him. It felt oddly safe. Secure. So, he let himself relax and that was apparently the right move, because Caiden's touch slipped lower again, until there was a palm pressed against Holland's cock. The groan that built in his throat escaped and Caiden grinned like he won something.

"Are you going to do more than tease me? I thought you'd made a promise to me at the bar," Holland said, proud that his voice didn't wobble too much.

"I did?"

Holland put his hand over Caiden's, pushing both their palms down while his cock twitched under their combined touch. It was brazen, yes, but Holland ached, and he trusted that if Caiden didn't want this, he would stop them. "Are you going to make good on that promise?"

Caiden's dark chuckle had Holland's hair standing on end, and the rush of electric pleasure that followed made him groan. "Damn, if you make these sounds now..." Caiden nudged him back. "I can't wait to see what you sound like in my bed."

There was no awkward tripping over each other to get to Caiden's bedroom. No frantic removing of clothes and frenzied touches. Caiden oh-so-sweetly led Holland down a dark hall, pointing out the bathroom before pulling him by the hands into the bedroom. The darkness didn't let him see his surroundings too well, but Holland didn't care. Caiden was already peeling out of his shirt and the play of his muscles and the wink of silver jewelry (in his ears, around his neck and fingers, through his nipples) lured him forward.

Holland let Caiden pull him down to the perfectly tucked-in

grey bedspread and he didn't stop to think or second guess himself. Especially not when Caiden was ridding him of his clothes and running his hands all over Holland's body.

He felt *wanted*. It was a burn of desire playing like flame against a cave of loneliness; one of his own making that had long lured Holland into that cold darkness and made him think it was what he needed. Solitude and his work.

Better late than never.

Holland slipped an arm under Caiden's back, relishing in all that warm skin now that they were both shirtless, and cradled his head in the palm of his hand. The angle gave Holland better access to Caiden's chest, and the moment he pressed his lips to Caiden's breastbone, the other man began to tremble. It was slight but steady, and paired with the gusty sigh Caiden let out, Holland figured he wasn't the only one waiting to find his way out of that lonely darkness.

"Is this okay?" Holland sought out Caiden's gaze in the darkness, his only light a small bedside touch lamp that threw a revolving set of colors against the brick walls.

"More than," Caiden breathed out. He reached down to run his fingers through Holland's hair and when he shivered at the touch, Caiden smiled. "Can I?"

It took Holland a minute (because his skin was buzzing and his heart was pounding hard and he could *feel* how warm he was, the burn of it spreading over his skin), but once he understood, he nudged up closer so Caiden could tug the elastic from his hair.

"Better?" Holland asked as his hair fell in his face and brushed the tops of his shoulders.

"You have no idea. It's fucking *gorgeous*," Caiden said. He craned up to meet Holland's lips, one hand buried in his hair, the other a solid, warm weight in the middle of Holland's back. "If I could sleep with your hair, I would."

Holland burst out laughing. "That's not a mental picture I needed."

"Well, you have it anyways. You're welcome."

Holland let out a snort. "I'll take 'Things I've Never Heard In Bed' for five hundred, Alex."

The warm hand that drew his face up was gentle in a way that took Holland by surprise, but the softness in Caiden's face didn't. For all his brawn, Caiden was gooey nougat in the center and Holland really liked that, but he was reading something else in the expression. Hesitation, maybe.

"So, before we go too far, how do you.... want to do this?" Caiden asked. "Cause I'm just glad you agreed to come home with me, and if you want me to blow you, or the other way around, that's more than good. And it's not that two bottoms or two tops can't go full cock-in-hole, but —"

Ah, that's what he'd been picking up on. It had been the same tightening of Caiden's jaw when he was concentrating at the mini golf course and at the pool table. He was still soft, still sweet, but now Holland understood. Nerves, like the ones that had Caiden rambling in the truck. His own had been doused in the flames of desire, and Caiden wasn't saying *stop* or *no*, but it was enough to have Holland pulling him up so they were face to face, both sitting up.

"I heard *if* a lot more than what you said to me just now," Holland said softly. "I'm nervous as hell, Caiden. But I only want to be here if you're sure. And we do not have to sleep together. I won't think any different of you if you want to put on the brakes."

Caiden's expression twisted at that. "I don't want to stop."

"But?"

Caiden gave him the softest little smile and then pulled Holland back down on top of him. "The concern is sweet. And I'm kind of turned on by it, not gonna lie. So there's no *but*, just…" He kissed Holland's cheek, and his stubble sent pleasant little shivers skating across Holland's body. "I didn't always pause before sex. Maybe let some things go in the past, when I should have said something. You giving me that second to think and really be sure means a lot."

Holland's chest instantly went tight with emotion. "Caiden."

A single utterance of his name and Caiden practically melted against Holland, pitching forward into his arms to run his lips over Holland's throat. "Trust that I want this."

Caiden didn't stop until he was braced on his hands over Holland, wild, wavy hair brushing Holland's forehead, his eyes lit with rekindled *need*. "Then tell me what you want," Holland said.

"I want these off," Caiden replied, yanking at the waist of his jeans. "And if you're in, I want these legs wrapped around me while I fuck you."

"You figured me out awfully easily," Holland said, reaching up to press his thumb into Caiden's lower lip. Caiden immediately pulled Holland's thumb between his lips and sucked hard. Holland's cock twitched in response.

"You like being bossed around a little?" Caiden's smirk was dangerous, damn near filthy. When he got down on his left forearm to free up his right hand, Holland only gripped him harder. Caiden's fingers, now in his hair, tightened in response and they both groaned. "Get naked, pretty boy."

Holland smiled back, all teeth and fire. "Do it for me."

The minute Caiden had them both free of the rest of their clothes, his hands roamed again. Up Holland's legs to press his fingers into the sparse flesh around his hips, and just as Holland arched into the touch with a moan, Caiden skated his thumbs over Holland's nipples. The yelp he let out in response was deeply undignified but couldn't be helped.

"Found a sweet spot," Caiden purred. "Maybe I forgot to mention, but I'm a big fan of men who have sensitive nipples." And he flicked the barbell through his own right nipple, hissing at the contact. "It's a personal little thing I have."

Holland's only response was to squeeze Caiden with his thighs and reach up, hand in the air while his face wore the question. When Caiden nodded, Holland circled his nipple with his thumb. Caiden's little appreciative shiver just made him harder, more desperate.

"Get down here," Holland said, not even waiting until Caiden was horizontal over him to start licking and kissing his neck, his throat, anywhere he could reach. Caiden kissed him back, hard and deep and exactly the way Holland liked it.

Holland got so wrapped up in the way Caiden felt, his mind and body buzzing with desire, that he forgot about the hand in his hair. Didn't even think about it again until Caiden gave an experimental tug and he gasped, stuck somewhere between pain and pleasure.

"Found another one," Caiden whispered. "Has anyone ever counted all those sweet little spots, Holland? The ones that make you gasp like that?"

From nervous to this, Holland thought right before Caiden tugged again. This time, Holland arched into it, exposing his throat, and it took not even a second for Caiden to descend on him with lips and tongue. He was gentle along the fragile skin of Holland's neck, but the hand in his hair — so tight, so perfect, enough to make Holland *throb* with need — spoke of something more constrained.

Something wanting to be set loose.

Holland wanted all of it.

"Fuck me," he gasped as Caiden rolled his right nipple between his lips.

"Only if you stay the night," Caiden shot back. He'd raised his head only so much, just enough so Holland could see his dark, dark eyes.

"Yes, please."

"So polite." Caiden's smirk was all teasing heat. "I doubt you can hold onto that with my hand on your dick."

Holland wasn't even going to argue with that. "Not a fucking bit."

"Good."

There were the usual negotiations around limbs and lube. Caiden left the wrapped condom on the side table for easy reach, but he wasn't even fully settled on his knees between Holland's legs before he started an easy, slow stroke down Holland's cock.

It felt *so good* to have someone else touching him and Holland couldn't help but encourage Caiden, nearly egging him on. "Fuck, that's amazing," he groaned, hips twitching, his thighs tightly clenched around Caiden's hips. "I knew you'd be good with your hands."

When Caiden chuckled for what seemed like the hundredth time, Holland realized it really had been far too long. Not just with being in someone else's bed, but genuinely having *fun* together. The easy patter between them, the banter, how simply they fell in step with each other even when naked and sweating and sticky with lube.

Holland stared up at Caiden for a long moment, enraptured by his touch and everything about him. And of course that was the moment Caiden decided to be clever, dragging his fingers up and down Holland's cock in a way that lit him up from the inside.

"Going to be a quick thing if you keep doing that," Holland said, voice strained. He could feel the heat already snaking up his spine and pooling in the pit of his stomach and he wasn't *ready yet*. Not yet. Not so soon.

Caiden slowly removed his hand, only to give himself a few strokes. He was beautiful, all compact muscles and dark, thick hair across his chest to a trail that thinned out down his stomach. Caiden let him reach out and run his fingers through it, until it was Holland's hand around his cock and Caiden was braced over him, clean hand on the wall, his expression pinched with pleasure.

Caiden's breath stuttered as he bit out a few sharp curses, but he never took his gaze off Holland. It was *intense*. A massive turn-on. And that hot, needy feeling made him desperate. He fumbled for the condom, slippery fingers losing purchase on the foil and Caiden was quick enough to grab for it. In the few moments it took for Caiden to rip it open and roll the condom down his cock, Holland was able to settle into the pillows and plant his feet into the mattress.

Caiden's gaze was greedy as it raked over Holland's legs and the space he'd created between them. Holland felt the same way but couldn't find the words; they were too mixed up in a tumult of desire and attraction and the warmth of a complimentary spirit. He pulled Caiden down to him and claimed his mouth while Caiden pressed a wet finger against his entrance.

Holland let his eyes fall shut at that touch. There'd been a time when he would have pushed Caiden to stretch him quickly, when he'd craved that feeling of being breached and taken. But now that soft, easy press of a fingertip into his body, the slow, slick slide of it, was what he really wanted, and this right now was *perfect*.

And when he managed to look up, Caiden was staring down at him like their world had narrowed to just the two of them. It was the intimacy of it that had Holland shivering and clinging even harder to Caiden's shoulders and back.

"You feel good," Caiden whispered, lips brushing his ear. "Want me to keep going?"

"*Please*."

By the time Caiden had him opened up, Holland was a puddle on the bed, living in some middle distance between relaxed and so pent up he thought he might explode. He had one leg hooked around Caiden's thigh, the other tipped limply to the mattress, making Caiden say, "Okay, you never said you were *that* flexible. Jesus, Holland. I doubt I could get my knee even halfway to the bed."

Holland raised an eyebrow, smirking. "Impressed?"

"Very."

Holland pulled him down again and Caiden came willingly as he pressed inside. "So good," Caiden exhaled while he let Holland shift around, getting used to the stretch.

"If you think that's good..." Holland brought his other leg up to trap Caiden between his thighs, tipped his hips up, and said, "Move."

Caiden *moved*. He was all short, powerful thrusts that made his gut clench and sent his heart into his throat. Holland clung to him, dug his fingers into Caiden's wavy hair, scratched down his back and made Caiden hiss appreciatively.

Caiden had been right. It was *so good*. The man was practically taking him apart and Holland knew he'd be sweaty and spent afterwards.

When Caiden reached down to stroke Holland's cock, he batted the hand away teasingly. "You've got other things….to focus on." The last few words came out on a gasp because Caiden nailed his prostate and Holland saw stars, felt liquid fire slip down his spine and it brought him so close to the edge far too quickly. Yeah, getting off was fun, but the physical connection, the closeness, was what he'd been craving for far too long.

"Just means I can do this." Caiden cupped his jaw and drew him into a kiss.

If he could have swooned…well, this was better. Much, much better. Especially because now that Caiden was figuring out how to make him gasp and squirm, he'd made it his sole mission and was doing a damn fine job of it.

"*Fuck*, Caiden."

"No shit." Caiden had his face shoved against Holland's neck now, his every breath warm against Holland's skin, and it was that extra little bit of sensory overload that would drag Holland over the edge. "Damn. I usually go longer than this."

"Don't." He nudged Caiden up until they could look at each other, which made him slow his thrusts. "There's no…magical first time. It's just us."

Caiden's brow pinched and just when he thought Caiden might protest, he nodded instead and said, "Yeah, okay, but you're getting off first."

And he fucked Holland like he really fucking goddamn *meant it*. Headboard into the wall, bed jolting, so good Holland felt his nerves pop and spark to life like a lightning rod until he came with a sharp groan. He was still shivering and panting when Caiden followed him down.

Caiden barely managed to roll off him before Holland pulled him back in. "I'll shove us both in the shower in a minute," he said. "Get your ass back here."

Caiden grinned. "Definitely not objecting to that." He tossed the condom and handed Holland some tissues, then binned it all and curled up next to Holland. "You still staying?"

Holland turned on his side so they were face to face. "Only if you want me to. I don't want to —"

Caiden cut him off with a kiss that was almost syrupy-slow and twice as sweet. "Then you're staying. And you still owe me that massage."

Holland laughed and pulled him in closer, until there was no space between their bodies. "Feel free to cash in that IOU whenever you want."

Chapter 10

CAIDEN

"Ouch."

Caiden, who had been kind of awake for a few moments, immediately rolled over to find Holland shaking out his hand. The knuckles were a little pink, but Holland's cheeks were red. He put two and two together. "You stretched and smacked your knuckles into the bed? Or the wall?"

"The headboard. So...the same thing, pretty much."

Caiden took quick stock of his bedroom. The morning light hadn't quite filtered in through those annoying but always present spots in the blinds; the ones that never quite seamlessly closed. So it was probably before seven. The blinds were cheap things that had come with the apartment a few years back and he'd never bothered to replace them because after a long, hard day at work, the minute his head hit the pillow, he was out.

He cast a look over at Holland. If this was going to be a thing - if, and he really hoped it would be - he'd need new blinds. He could deal with a bit of light in the morning, but maybe Holland wasn't as heavy a sleeper.

"I can hear your gears churning," Holland said, finally done rubbing his knuckles. He also turned on his side, all long limbs and warm skin, and the rush of pleasure Caiden had all but bathed in last night tried to valiantly come back. Mostly in the form of morning wood.

"I do that sometimes," Caiden said while reaching out to brush his fingers across Holland's arm. "Some people have shower thoughts. I have early morning ones, because I'm usually too tired to have big thoughts at the end of the day."

"Hmmm." Holland inched closer. Shit, he was even gorgeous all sleep and sex mussed with deep creases in his face from the pillows. Life really wasn't fair. "Care to share? You don't have to, but I'm a good listener."

"Okay, but you can't laugh."

"Scout's honor." Holland gave a little two-fingered salute. "I don't know. I wasn't a scout of any kind. But I actually am a good listener."

"I was thinking if this becomes a..." Caiden motioned between them. "A thing. You and me. I might need to replace those blinds. They're old and annoying. But I hate messing with house stuff. It's like the *last* thing I want to do, even though I know how to."

Holland's expression became curious. "Just home improvement stuff? I'm not hand-waving away your dislike but —"

Caiden wanted to smack himself. "I'm an idiot. No, I meant...shit. The blinds let in light and if you're gonna be here, it seems rude to have light coming in when you're trying to sleep. And I'm saying *if* cause I really liked last night. Really, really did. But that's a lot of pressure and it's early and —"

Holland cut him off with a kiss. Morning breath be damned (and the guy didn't really have much anyways). "I'm not trying to stop you from talking," he said as he pulled away after a few seconds. "It's reassurance. About everything."

"Oh." Okay, now he felt a little too warm. As in, could feel his fucking *ears* burning. "I'm still changing those things. They're stupid and they rattle if you so much as breathe on them."

And then Holland's lips were sliding over his jaw and down his throat and Caiden lost track of things for a bit.

The room was bordering on too cold, but two shirtless guys down to their skivvies under heavy quilts kept things plenty warm. With Holland now so close and so *alive* beside him, Caiden never wanted to leave, even if it was to adjust the thermostat out in the hall.

"Christ," Caiden breathed when Holland got his lips around his left nipple. The barbells had been one of many things he'd done simply because he wanted to, and admittedly they'd turned into a bit of an obsession for most of his lovers. But Holland knew how to light him up with just a few touches and was well on his way to driving Caiden mad.

Almost too late, Caiden remembered Holland liked a bit of hair pulling, but when he reached down to run his fingers through it, Holland looked up. "Let me make you feel good, Caiden."

"Oh, fuck you," Caiden replied, which Holland thankfully took how he meant. (Aka a massive fucking compliment.) "You did plenty of that last night."

Holland shrugged. His touch was light over Caiden's ribs, bordering on ticklish, and when Caiden squirmed against him, Holland just sighed and crawled on top of him. "Okay, fine. But I *want* to do this. I can concede your point and still want to taste you."

"How the fuck do you that?" His words came out a little staggered, a little halted, because Holland went back to licking around the barbell like it was a lollipop. Caiden thought his spine might melt. Just a little.

"Do what?"

"Sound...*shit, Holland.*" Caiden's brain stuttered to a stop as Holland put the lightest bit of pressure around his nipple. *With his fucking teeth.* "Fuck. Oh, fuck you. Sound...I don't know, proper and posh and shit and be hot at the same time."

He was quickly understanding that particular grin of Holland's; part pleased with himself sprinkled with a tinge of mischief. It was hot enough to actually melt his brain. "It's a blessing and a curse," Holland said before turning his attention to Caiden's other nipple.

Caiden was now *very* awake, and his very present erection was probably jabbing Holland in the stomach. Or, it should have been, given their height difference, but as Holland moved to fully blanket him, Caiden realized he was hard, too. That was a cock pressing into his thigh and those were Holland's delicious hips making the smallest of movements.

"You're...getting off on this," Caiden panted. Now he did push his fingers through Holland's hair, earning him a soft groan followed by a louder one as he gently pulled on the thick blonde strands. "Perfect pairing between us, I guess."

"Service top meets flexible bottom?"

Caiden grinned at him. "Flexible in more ways than one. And you can't say that without me thinking of at least five ways to test how bendy you are."

Holland repaid his remark by reaching down to fondle his balls. The microfiber boxer-briefs he wore were no shield against that burning touch, but Caiden let himself fall into it. He let Holland touch him, kiss him, and groan softly in his ear as they gently rocked together.

No hurry. Nowhere to go. Just body heat and skin and the low, pulsing throb of easy pleasure.

While coffee brewed and Caiden had put some bread in the toaster oven, he joined Holland on the couch, but only after handing him a framed photo.

"I didn't want to be that goofy cliche in the movie, the one where the lover is roaming around the house the next morning and sees the picture that explains it all."

Caiden let Holland take a good look at the photo of him and his grandfather in front of the very pirate ship he'd conquered last night and watched the math add up. It didn't take long.

"I know, I look like *me* even as a kid," Caiden said lightly. "And hold onto that, I'll get the coffee."

He came back with two steaming mugs – his with cream, Holland's black with sugar – and settled down on the couch. "So, my grandad was this nutty professor-style scientist," Caiden began. "He had a bunch of patents by the time he was twenty-five but had never really found a way to make money from his inventions. When he married my grandma, they started a standing date kind of thing and one night was at the local mini golf place. Calvin, my grandad, had never played, but that one night was all it took for him to get hooked."

Caiden paused to sip his coffee and Holland closed any gap in the conversation as easily as he took brilliant photos. "I'm guessing he got obsessed."

"Bingo. And obsessed is putting it mildly. He started designing: traps, decorations, whole mazes, even had this one plan that never panned out with lasers and motion sensors. If he'd had today's technology, he could have nailed it, I think."

Holland motioned toward the picture frame now nestled in Caiden's lap. "And that's you and him in front of the pirate ship. So, it was his invention?"

Caiden couldn't help but smile at that. Any time he got to talk about his grandad, there was this rush of fond, colorful memories that time hadn't yet withered to black and white. "One of many. And the only one I couldn't beat, until last night."

"Caiden." Holland was instantly leaning in, expression soft in a way that, for some reason, made Caiden's throat tighten. "I can't believe you shared that with me."

Caiden tried to laugh it off. He really did. But it came out all strangled and he covered it up by drinking more coffee. The hot liquid scalded his tongue and only made him swallow hard. So much for playing it cool. "I...you're not angry with me? I mean, I should have just done it on my own but every time I tried, it never worked. I thought if I had someone with me it would be easier. Maybe. And I'm not trying to usurp what was a really wonderful night..."

He stopped rambling when Holland reached over to squeeze his hand. The sincerity in his eyes was only matched by his gentle words. "I'm *honored* you shared that with me. But I clearly have a standard to live up to now." Caiden gave him a confused look and Holland laughed. "Well, clearly now I need to beat that damn pirate ship, too, so I'll need to consult with an expert."

"Oh my god, that's the cheesiest thing I've ever heard," Caiden groaned as Holland kept laughing. "But also the sweetest."

"I try."

"I'd say you do more than *try*, hot stuff."

A few weeks later

"Am I the first one to see it?" Caiden asked as he took the wrapped package from Holland. He'd swung by Holland's place to pick him up for dinner and waiting for him had been a fresh-off-the-printer copy of the calendar.

Holland actually ducked his head at that, a sly smile on his face. "As far as photography subjects go, yes. It's only been me, my assistant, and the printer who have seen it so far. I dropped some copies off at Laurent's office, but he won't be back in until Monday so..."

Holland motioned for him to open the calendar and Caiden carefully unwrapped it. He felt strangely nervous, even though he, just like all the other photography subjects, had approved the final photos.

"Oh," he said when he saw his image above the July calendar. He'd let Holland pick the photo to be featured from his approved ones, and to his surprise, it was the very first photo they'd shot, aside from that test headshot Holland had taken. He was in jeans and a reflective vest sans shirt, one booted foot on a shovel with his other hand on his hip. Caiden remembered taking the photo, remembered feeling out of place until Holland had, in that easy way of his, gotten him to relax.

He looked *good*. He looked at ease. And whatever had inspired Holland to use that photo, Caiden was grateful for, because it *worked.*

Holland had asked each subject to write up why they offered to be featured, and seeing his words in print was a little unreal, but also a moment that Caiden realized was one he should be proud of.

I'm honored to be considered a local hero. I didn't think of myself like that in any way, but it was pointed out to me how much me and everyone at GreenWorks Landscaping does for the community. From the community gardens we help maintain to the pro bono work we do for those working on neighborhood clean-ups, it's a real pleasure to know that I'm out there helping and making the city a little bit brighter. But I'm also just honored because this charity and Color Run efforts helped my sister when she was going through a severe illness as a kid, and I'd like to pass on that spirit of charity wherever possible.

While Caiden was reading, Holland had come up behind him, his warmth an anchor to help Caiden stay grounded while he could feel tears stinging the backs of his eyes. "Thank you," he whispered, tilting his head back so Holland could kiss his temple. "I feel crazy for even thinking this, but you just...you get me. And that's not to say things can't change but having you with me feels right."

Holland's arms tightened around him. "Come upstairs with me for a second. I want to show you something."

Caiden followed Holland to his loft bedroom but when Holland tugged him gently to the photo wall, he realized immediately what was different. The photos had been grouped a certain way before, and many were still in place from the last time he'd seen them (through bleary eyes a few mornings ago, when he'd stayed over).

But the upper left corner was different. Holland was a shutter-bug no matter the day or time or activity, and they'd taken several pictures together over the dates they'd had. So, there were all the photos of them, pinned to the board in a tidy cluster. In the center was the shot Holland had taken of him on their first date, of him in the truck looking out of the windshield. But there were also two shots with only Holland in them; shots Caiden had taken, the ones Holland had promised him on that first date.

Caiden's favorite was one he'd shot from below, Holland staring down at him with a mix of lazy smugness and pure sex. The man was a natural born model but preferred to be behind the camera, and Caiden felt honored that he'd been trusted with that expensive equipment, but also with such an intimate moment. And knowing he'd been the cause of that look on Holland's face...it still made him shiver.

It all, somehow, felt like an age ago. And like yesterday, and like their tomorrow, too.

Caiden stared at the board, then moved to stand in front of their little grouping of photos, and when Holland took his hand, he squeezed back. "It's perfect," he said. "I feel really special. Like, to a degree that I don't have words for."

He could feel Holland's gaze on him, and when he looked up, Holland's soft, syrupy smile nearly tipped him over the edge of feeling too damn much. "I don't have the right words for it," Caiden admitted as he pulled Holland into a hug. "But it's one of the sweetest things anyone's ever done for me. Seriously."

"I'm glad you like it." Holland tipped up his chin with a finger, and when Caiden leaned into the kiss, the unspoken between them felt very much like a promise.

About the author

Halli Starling is a queer librarian fascinated by the occult and strange history. She lives in Michigan with her spouse, feline supervisors, and is always surrounded by books.
When not writing, she co-hosts The Human Exception podcast and plays D&D.

For updates on her writing and more, follow Halli on Instagram @hallistarling.
Website: hallistarlingbooks.com